Praise for Kate Perry's Novels

"Perry's storytelling skills just keep getting better and better!"

—*Romantic Times Book Reviews*

"Can't wait for the next in this series...simply great reading. Another winner by this amazing author."

—*Romance Reviews Magazine*

"Exciting and simply terrific."

—*Romancereviews.com*

"Kate Perry is on my auto buy list."

—*Night Owl Romance*

"A winning and entertaining combination of humor and pathos."

—*Booklist*

Other Titles by Kate Perry

Loved By You

Kate Perry

Phoenix Rising Enterprise, Inc.

Thank you.

I can't tell you how much your awesome notes, funny comments, and general enthusiasm means to me. Writing is HARD, and some days it's only your encouragement and knowing how much you're looking forward to the next story that keeps me going. Thank you. LOVED BY YOU is dedicated to you. I'm drinking a toast to you and your own happily ever after!

Also, special thanks to Julia Enders, who thought Laurel Heights needed a pig. Ante Up is way smaller than James, but James is not San Francisco sized. Wink.

Chapter One

*T*HE MOMENT KT stepped into her parents' kitchen she knew she'd made a mistake.

Her sister Bijou sat at the Henry VIII table, reading a magazine. Their little mother Lara washed grapes at the sink, her back turned toward KT. A tranquil, normal scene.

And so deceptive because there was nothing normal about her family.

KT looked around, not sure whether she should enter or run away. Lately Lara had a mission: to find KT a boyfriend. She wouldn't have been surprised if her mom had a man hidden somewhere for her.

Cup of coffee or back away quietly?

Back away. She took a careful step back.

As if a radar went off, her mom looked over her shoulder. "Karma, sweeting, there you are."

She winced like she always did when she heard

the name her parents had saddled her with. Who named their kid Karma?

New Age hippy rockers like Anson and Lara. Fortunately, she could just go by KT. She'd met Chris and Gwyneth's kid Apple at one of her parents' parties, and she'd immediately felt sorry for the little thing. She started to wonder how life named Apple would be worse, but was distracted by the militant light in her mom's eyes.

"Stop hovering in the doorway, Karma." Lara motioned to a chair. "Sit next to your sister. I want to talk to you."

Bijou glanced up from the issue of Rolling Stone she was flipping through and gave her a look that said run away.

Coffee, KT mouthed silently.

Bijou pushed a half-full cup across the table toward her.

That was why she loved her sister—Bijou had her back. Bijou was three years younger and completely opposite in every way, but they'd always been close. KT credited her sister for that. At twenty-seven, Bijou had it together. She knew what she wanted: to be on the cover of Rolling

Stone. And she had a plan to get it.

KT? Not so much. Especially since Jamila, the singer she'd been writing songs for, fired her last year. She told herself she had everything she needed. She lived in the carriage house at the back of her parents' property in peace. She had her piano. She had good friends. She was happy. Sort of.

Except for when her mom was trying to pimp her out.

She'd taken the enforced break from writing pop songs to work on something she really cared about: a piano concerto. It was a departure, but she loved the challenge. She had no idea what she was going to do with it once she finished it. She certainly wasn't going to play it herself. Performing made her puke. She could feel bile rising in her throat at the mere thought.

That'd been a bone of contention for the past year between her and her parents—and by "her parents" she meant her mom. KT did her best to avoid the main house. Usually. Until she ran out of coffee in her cottage and became desperate.

She cradled Bijou's coffee to her chest and sidled away. "I need to get back now, so I'll just—"

"Sit, Karma." Her mother pointed to the chair. Then she frowned. "What on earth are you wearing?"

KT glanced down. "Clothes."

Bijou grinned. "Better that than plastic wrap, Mom."

"I don't know. I might prefer plastic wrap." Her mother shook her head, clearly dismayed. "Really, Karma. You look like a lumberjack."

She tugged at her shirt. "It's cold today."

Still shaking her head, Lara said, "Karma, I need to discuss something with you."

Her sister gave her a commiserating look and pushed out the seat next to her. "Maybe you should sit down."

Crossing her arms, she gave her sister a baleful look and then returned her attention to her mom. "Can this wait? I'm in the middle of something."

"What could you possibly be in the middle of, Karma? You have no life."

"Ouch," Bijou said as she flipped a page.

KT nudged her sister with her foot. "I have a life. I like my life."

Her mother crossed her arms, looking intractable. "You don't have a life. You're a hobbit."

"I think you mean hermit, Mom," Bijou corrected mildly.

"Semantics." Lara waved a heavily jewelled hand. "The point here is that Karma isn't living up to her potential."

Her mom hated that she wrote songs for other people, but KT couldn't imagine being in the limelight. Bijou craved it. KT began to hyperventilate thinking about having to perform in front of just a handful of people.

Bijou set the magazine aside. "Mom, since you're so busy preparing for your benefit concert in three weeks, maybe you and KT can discuss this later."

Lara smiled. "I'm so happy you brought up the concert, love."

KT and Bijou exchanged a look. Bijou was the one to ask, "What about the concert?"

"Your father and I have been discussing the situation." She faced KT. "We were thinking of evicting you from the cottage."

"What?" She blinked at her mom, stunned.

The cottage was hers. She'd lived in it since she'd turned eighteen.

"But I knew that wouldn't work," her mom continued. "You'd just find another dank, dark place to hole yourself up in and then we'd never see you. And you still wouldn't do anything with your music. So we came up with a different solution."

"Solution? There's no problem!" KT protested. "I'm happy where I am."

Lara arched her brow. "Are you?"

"Yes." Pretty much. She liked being alone. Or rather, she didn't like people. Most people—there were a few people like Bijou and her friends Scott, Griffin, and Nicole who she did enjoy spending time with.

Her mom studied her silently, then shook her head, her long blond hair waving gently. "I don't think you are happy, Karma. I don't even know what you do out there in the cottage."

"I'm composing."

"For what reason? To plaster your walls with music no one's ever going to hear? You're not even selling your songs anymore, Karma."

"That's not my fault."

"Yes, it is," her mother said gently. "Jamila fired you."

"Only because she couldn't stand the truth."

Bijou cleared her throat. "You told her she was singing it all wrong."

"She was," KT insisted.

"But maybe you didn't have to tell her a dog could do a better job," her sister suggested mildly.

She shrugged, crossing her arms. "I can't help it if she can't take constructive criticism."

"Whatever the cause, Karma," her mother continued, "you can't continue living this half-life. You're thirty. You should be over your Saturn return by now. Which is why I'm going to do this."

Her heart froze in fear. "What are you doing?"

"We want you to be part of the concert."

"Hell no." She never played in front of a crowd. Ever. Occasionally, she played with her friend Griffin or Bijou, but always in the privacy of her own studio. She knew her parents eavesdropped sometimes, but they loved her no matter what, so they didn't count.

KT began pacing, sickly sweat breaking out on her forehead as she imagined a million eyes fo-

cused on her, waiting for her to screw up. "You know I don't perform in public."

"It's time for that to change. It's time to let the old fears go, Karma."

It may have happened twenty-six years ago, but the fears didn't feel old at all. Just the thought of being on stage brought everything back in a rush: her mom pushing her toward the piano, the feeling of her lungs being crushed from the weight of everyone's stare, the clumsiness of her fingers, the beginning of the tittering laughter as she stumbled on the keys. Just like she was still in that room, in front of all her parents' friends and colleagues, she began to sweat, her voice paralyzed.

Her mother walked up to her and reached up to touch her face. "You have a gift, Karma. Forget having perfect pitch and being talented at every instrument you pick up. Your voice is heaven sent. It's criminal how you aren't using it. Do you know how many people would kill to have it? And no one's ever heard it."

She shrugged, trying to pretend that she wasn't affected by her mom's words. "Nothing's going to convince me to play in the concert."

"I was afraid you'd say that." Lara took a deep breath and straightened her already perfect posture. "That's why your father and I decided that if you don't perform at our concert, neither can Bijou."

"What?" KT and Bijou exclaimed together.

Lara lifted her chin. "You give me no choice, Karma. It's you and Bijou or neither one of you. You decide."

KT turned to her sister, who looked stricken. She knew how important this concert was to Bijou. Her sister had worked her ass off to get noticed on her own merit without cashing in on their parents' name. Her star had been steadily rising until The Incident last year, as they'd been calling it.

But Bijou had bounced back and was ready to take her place in rock history, and this concert was going to launch her. Unless she was banned from being in it.

"Crap," KT said succinctly, slumping onto a seat.

"Yeah." Looking shell-shocked, Bijou set the magazine down and faced their mom. "I don't understand. What did I do to rate this?"

"Nothing, love." Lara ran a loving hand over her younger daughter's hair, affection glowing from her expression. "This has nothing to do with you and everything to do with Karma. It's for her own good."

"So you're punishing me?" Bijou asked.

"You know how much she loves you. She'll do anything for you."

"But I won't do that," KT interjected.

Her mom ignored her. "The only way Karma will overcome her stage fright is if she has a stake that's high enough to encourage her to change her pattern. We all know how hard you've been working for this concert, Bijou, and how much it means to you, especially with what happened with that awful Bryland boy. If anything is going to inspire Karma, it's her love for you."

Bijou shook her head. "KT isn't going to get on stage. She can't even tune her guitar in front of a handful of people without freezing or getting sick."

Lara patted Bijou's arm. "Then I suggest you help your sister get over her fear."

"This is unbelievable." KT waved her arm, not

caring that the coffee sloshed onto her shirt. "You can't do this to Bijou."

"Yes, we can," Lara said firmly. "Which leads me to the second thing I want to talk to you about."

"Is this where you take away my car next?" Bijou asked wryly.

"Don't be silly, Bijou. This has nothing to do with you." Lara speared KT a look. "Your sex life."

"What sex life?" her sister chimed in.

She shot Bijou a glare. "Brat."

Lara came to stand toe-to-toe with her. "I invited a man over for you to meet."

"Mom." She grabbed her hair at the roots. "I don't need you to pimp me out."

"Apparently you do. You never leave the cottage, Karma," her mom said when she continued to protest. "You're selling yourself short. You have so much in you and you bottle it up. So we're giving you a life enema."

"Geez, Mom." She began to pace. "I'm not performing, and I'm not dating anyone you throw at me. I'm perfectly capable of finding my own boyfriend."

"Are you?" Lara said with an arch of her brow.

She crossed her arms. She didn't want to date

anyone. She had a concerto to finish. She was busy.

Lara took the forgotten coffee cup out of KT's hands. "He's coming over later. Don't disappear. And, for goodness's sake, Karma, change your shirt."

They watched speechless as their mom floated out of the kitchen.

"I didn't see that Mack truck coming," her sister said.

Neither did KT, but she wasn't letting it run her over. She hoped.

Chapter Two

BIJOU TAYLOR MEASURED her life in two periods, before and after Brice Bryland.

Forget that backstabbing cockroach. She breathed in as she squeezed her right butt in the lunge, trying to focus on the music playing over the speakers rather than her bitterness.

It was hard—she had a lot of bitterness toward Brice. Of course, it was warranted. After the way he'd pretended to like her, only to steal the song she wrote, she couldn't imagine feeling any other way.

She shook her head and switched legs. She needed to focus on positive things. Being negative wasn't going to help her achieve her goal of being on the cover of Rolling Stone by herself and not as part of a feature on her parents.

She had all her goals and dreams set on this concert. She'd wanted her success to be based on her own merit not her parents' name, but after last

year with Brice and being dropped by the label, she wasn't averse to using their benefit concert as a platform.

She was going to nail it, too. All she ever wanted was to be a rock star.

Being the daughter of the legendary duo, Anson and Lara, was both a blessing and a curse. Not that she'd change anything. She adored her parents, especially her dad. Somehow, incredibly, they'd provided her and her sister a grounded, nurturing environment despite the touring and fame.

She glanced at her father who was lying on a bench, fiddling with his iPhone instead of working out. "You doing okay over there, Daddy?"

"Just dandy, Ruby Red." He waved a hand over his head, his attention never wavering from his phone. "Just taking a second to recover."

A flood of humor and love filled her chest. He was adorable, more like a geeky older guy than a rock star. Unlike his contemporaries, he was a sweet, loving family man. She loved that he still called her Ruby Red. He'd forever been telling her she was a "magnificent jewel."

She had him and her mom to thank for the

person she was, from her looks to her talent. Her talent was a given, although she knew KT blew her out of the water where that was concerned. Her looks—well, she played up the basics her parents had passed down.

Not that she looked anything like them. Her mom and dad were both small. She and KT towered over them, apparently throwbacks to some recessive Amazonian gene in their line. Except for their eyes—they both had their mother's hazel eyes.

The one thing Anson and Lara had passed on was their love for music and their talent. Bijou had always wanted to follow in their footsteps. She lived for the adoring roar of a crowd and seeing their rapt expression as she sang.

KT? Not so much. Her sister preferred to be behind the scenes. Not that Bijou could blame her, not from what she'd heard about that dinner party when KT was four years old. Bijou shuddered, imagining the scene she'd been way too young to witness.

She kind of understood why their mom was doing this. She knew Lara had always felt guilty about that night; obviously she was trying to correct a wrong. Bijou just wished her mom hadn't coldcocked her. Because that was what it felt like, just like when Brice had stolen her song.

"You need spotting?" her dad asked absently, out of the blue.

"I'm fine." She glanced over at him as she stepped out of the lunge. "How about you?"

"I've got it all covered."

From her perspective, it looked like the only thing he had covered was Angry Birds. She grabbed her workout towel and blotted. "Are you doing more reps?"

"Of course. I haven't maintained this physique by being a sloth." He patted the small belly he'd started to grow in his sixties.

"You're my role model." Bijou got on the floor to do a set of tricep push-ups, remembering how she'd thought Brice was so much like her dad when she'd first met him.

Wrong. So wrong.

Gritting her teeth, she held the pose low, and then painfully pushed up. She'd been a fool about Brice. A double fool, because he'd not only broken her heart, but he'd stolen the song she'd composed for the two of them to sing.

KT had called him an asshole. Actually, KT still called him an asshole.

Bijou smiled, warmed with the love that she always felt when she thought of her sister. She'd witnessed her friend Rosalind's relationship with her sisters, so she didn't take her closeness with KT for granted.

She couldn't disagree with their mom. KT really was wasting away in the carriage house. Her sister wasn't much of a performer, even if she didn't get stage fright, but she was an amazing composer and musician. And her voice. If Bijou hadn't been so secure in her own talents, she'd have been bitterly jealous that KT got the angel's lungs.

The door to the workout room opened and the object of her thoughts walked in. Which struck her odd because her sister avoided anything hard. "Are you working out?" Bijou asked.

"Hell no." Looking at her like she was insane, KT walked to the refrigerator in the corner. "I'm out of sparkling water in the carriage house. Hey Dad."

Their dad groaned like he was benching two-hundred instead of his four-ounce phone.

Bijou watched her sister pull out a bottle and shook her head. "First coffee, now water. Maybe you should go shopping."

KT shrugged as she uncapped it. "It's easier this way. The main house is closer than Whole Foods."

"You're the laziest person I know."

"I have no problem with that role." She pointed with the water bottle. "Better than kicking my ass just to look good."

"It's a part of my career." Elbows in a stable triangle, she slowly lifted her legs into a headstand. "I have to look good."

KT made a face. "I'm not going to bust my balls just to look a certain way for my public."

"You don't have a public."

"And I like it that way."

"Well," their dad said, heaving himself up from the bench like his muscles just couldn't handle it any longer. He stretched his arms out and groaned. "I'll leave you two girls to do your thing. Thanks for the workout, Ruby Red."

"Any time, Daddy."

He stopped to give KT a kiss on the cheek before shuffling out.

"It's so cute that you guys are workout partners," KT said after the door closed. "Does he ever actually exercise?"

"Of course not. I think he comes up here to make Mom happy."

"Speaking of making Mom happy, I came up with a solution." KT smiled in her usual, confident way. "I just need to show her that I'm living up to my potential, right? She doesn't care what I do as long as I'm fulfilled."

"How are you going to do that?"

"I'm going to get a job."

Bijou laughed, tightening her abs to keep from falling out of her pose.

"What?" KT frowned. "You don't think I can find a job?"

"Oh, you can find a job, I just don't think anyone would hire you. And don't say Starbucks would," she said, cutting off her sister. "They might, but they'd fire you the instant a customer pissed you off and you told them to shove it."

KT frowned. "You're right."

Of course she was. She knew her sister.

"I'll just have to do other things," KT said.

"Like?"

"I don't know. I'll think of something."

Mom was right—she was going to have to help KT get her ass on stage. "You better come up with a more concrete plan than that, or else get ready to strut your stuff."

Her sister shuddered. "Don't threaten me."

"I'm just warning you how it's going to be." She levelled a look at KT, who slouched.

"I'm not going to let you down, Bijou. I'll show Mom I'm living my life so she'll relent and stop punishing you."

The door opened. "Bijou, love, are you in here?" their mom called out.

KT looked at her and then dove behind the counter of the little kitchen area, ducking behind the cabinets.

Bijou arched her brow at her sister, who waved her hand madly. She dropped out of her headstand and began to do bicycle crunches. "In here, Mom."

Lara glided in, her flowing dress trailing her thin frame. Their mom had an ethereal type of beauty that became more finely honed instead of decaying as she got older. "Bijou, have you seen your sister? She's not in the carriage house."

She resisted glancing to her right. "I haven't seen her in a bit. Why?"

"I invited someone over to meet her." Her mom checked her watch. "He's waiting in the living room, and I haven't been able to find her. I don't want her to stand him up like she did the nice boy I invited over yesterday."

She darted a glance at her sister, who shook her head so hard her hair flipped over her face. Sighing, Bijou returned her attention to Lara. "I'll look for her, Mom."

"Thank you, love." She blew a kiss and left.

After checking to make sure the coast was clear, KT scrambled out from behind the counter. "Later, dude."

"Wait." Flipping onto her stomach, she grabbed her sister's leg as she rushed by. "Where are you going?"

"To Scott's. Duh."

"Scott's on his honeymoon."

"It doesn't matter. I'll go hide in his house. Half the time I never see him anyway."

"What about the guy in the living room?"

"You go see him."

Bijou shook her head, sitting up. "He's here for you."

"Then he's going to be waiting a long time," KT said over her shoulder as she strode out of the gym.

"You owe me," she yelled after her sister, getting up from the floor. "Big."

All she heard was the quiet whoosh of the door closing.

"Fine." She drank a swig of water, grabbed her hand towel, and dabbed at her face on her way downstairs.

Bijou stumbled on the unsuspecting guy wandering in the hallway looking at the platinum records lining the entryway. She pasted a smile on her face and went to tell him KT wasn't interested in dating him, cursing her mom for feeding these poor men to the wolves like this.

Though this one, at least, looked good from

behind. His faded jeans molded to him perfectly, and his black shirt showed off wide shoulders.

He looked up as she approached, and she was struck still by his ultra-blue eyes. She blinked, feeling like she'd been slammed into a wall.

Only then she saw the details — the thick leather necklace around his neck, his artfully messed hair, and just enough five o'clock shadow to look disreputable without being slovenly — and she frowned. He was so her type.

Which made him all wrong for her.

She straightened her spine and headed for him.

He pointed to her parents' records as she approached. "This is amazing," he said.

She glanced at the gleaming gold and platinum discs. One day . . . One day. She nodded. "It's a life's work."

"It's a good amount of work." He smiled at her. "Are you Karma?"

She laughed, and then she laughed more; the thought of her being her sister was so ridiculous.

"You have a great laugh, even when it's at my expense." Still smiling, looking more interested, he held his hand out. "Will Shaw."

"Bijou Taylor, Karma's younger and more charming sister." She shook his hand, ignoring the shivers that went up her arm and down her spine. She let go and stepped back.

He looked beyond her. "Is Karma on the way?"

"No."

He didn't bat a lash. "Will she be on her way?"

"I'll just be upfront, because you seem like a nice guy." Bijou put her hand on his arm. Strong. Ropy. Hot. She shook her head to clear it rather than in reply to his question. "KT sent me to run interference. I'm sure if she met you, she'd like you, but she's not interested right now."

He frowned. "Lara led me to believe that KT had signed on to the idea."

"Mom can be overly optimistic." So he wouldn't feel bad, she added, "It's not you."

"It's her?" he asked with a grin.

"Totally. You're attractive and everything—"

"You think so?"

She sighed. "Unfortunately."

He arched his brow.

"But don't get any ideas," she said quickly, raising her hand, "because I'm not interested in dating anyone now, either."

"So the Taylor sisters are both resistant to relationships."

She frowned. "You make us seem like we have issues."

"Everyone has issues, it's just a matter of how they manifest."

"What are you, a psychologist?"

"A psychiatrist, actually. I have a private practice specializing in performance anxiety."

Bijou gaped. "No way."

"Why not?" he asked with a curious tip of his head.

"Therapists aren't supposed to look like male strippers."

He laughed. "I'm going to take that as a compliment."

Bijou blushed. She never blushed. She hadn't even blushed when she was a little girl.

Then what he said caught her attention. "You're a performance anxiety therapist?" she asked.

"For athletes, mainly, but I also deal with actors and musicians."

"My mother didn't have you come over to date KT, did she? She wanted to hire you to help her."

"But it's flattering that you thought I could date your sister."

She tossed her towel aside. "Let's talk therapy."

"Do you need help?"

"Of course not, but KT does." She slipped her arm through his. "Let's get out of here and find a quiet place to talk."

**Grounds for Thought was the logical place to take Will.

In Los Angeles, Bijou had gone to the same café every day for three years, and they always looked at her like she was a stranger. She'd been frequenting Grounds for Thought for the two weeks since she'd been home, and she felt like she belonged.

As they entered, she waved to Eve, who owned the bookstore café, and her friends Gwen and Lola. They all smiled and called out to her as she and Will headed to the counter.

"Friends?" Will asked softly as they approached the register.

"New friends." She smiled brightly at them. "Hey ladies!"

Lola leaned over and held her croissant up. "Did you come here to flaunt the fact that you've worked out and I'm eating a buttery pastry? Because I may have to kill you off in my next book."

Gwen frowned at her friend. "You write romance novels. There's no murder."

"There's always a first time."

Bijou grinned. Lola had a perfect body—whatever she was doing was working for her. "Would you feel better if I order a pastry, too?"

"Yes." Lola pointed at her but faced Gwen. "I love this woman. She gets it."

Laughing, Eve wiped the counter. "Lola has her priorities straight. What can I get you guys besides a treat?"

Gwen prodded Lola with her elbow. "I love when she offers people a 'treat.'"

"I know. I'd totally tap that if I didn't have Sam." Lola smiled at Bijou. "Treat is Eve's husband's name. He's hot."

Not as hot as Will. She glanced at him, hoping her face didn't give away her thoughts. "Share a

chocolate croissant with me?"

"Yes." He ordered a coffee for himself, and Bijou added an herbal tea for herself. Will paid for it despite her protests and then went to scope out a spot for them to sit.

Lola leaned across Gwen to whisper, "Okay, quick. Who is he, and are you doing him?"

"He's someone I just met, and no, I'm not doing him." She was tempted to go there, though, which was exactly why she wasn't going to think about it. Much.

"Bummer." Lola craned her neck to look at Will. "He has a great butt."

"What happened to Sam?" Gwen asked with a quirk of her eyebrow as she lifted her tiny espresso cup.

"Sam is my world. This is research."

Gwen laughed. Then she gasped and turned her big eyes onto Bijou. "Wait. You're a musician, right?"

"Right."

The woman leaned toward her, intense in a way that was unexpected given her bohemian appearance. "I chair the Purple Elephant, a foundation that gives kids a place to learn and create, and I have a girl who needs a piano teacher. Would you be interested in volunteering? It'd just be twice a week."

"I've never taught anyone anything, but I'd be glad to help." Bijou pursed her lips as an idea hit. Maybe she should pass this on to KT, as part of her reformation, even though she thought it was lame to try to con their mom into thinking KT was anything other than a hermit. "Actually, let me talk to my sister. She's looking for something like this."

"Great!" Gwen beamed at her as she took out a card from her clutch. "Have her contact me."

Will came up behind her right as she slipped the card into her sports bra. His eyes flicked to her cleavage, and she thought she saw a second of appreciation there, but he schooled his expression quickly. "I saved us the window seat," he said while picking up the drinks that Eve slid across the counter.

"I've got this." She took the croissant and smiled at the ladies. "See you guys later."

Lola winked at her, and they all looked at Will and laughed.

"Do I want to know what that was about?" he asked as they sat down.

"I doubt it." She grinned playfully as she angled her seat toward his.

He pushed her tea closer to her. "It seems like you're good friends. How long have you known them?"

"A couple weeks." She shrugged at his surprised look. "I live in LA normally, but I'm performing with my parents at their benefit concert in a few weeks, so I've been staying up here with them. I figured it was easier than commuting from Southern California."

Not to mention that she wanted to get away from the LA music scene because in the past month her song—the one Brice stole—had hit the charts and was everywhere. She'd needed to get away.

She realized Will Shaw was studying her. He looked so much like a bad boy, with his man jewelry and worn jeans—so much like Brice in some way. Except for the expression in his eyes. He looked at her like he could see all the way into her. "Want to tell me what's going on?" he asked.

For a second, she thought he meant about

Brice, and she stiffened. But then she realized he meant with her sister.

Relaxing, she nodded. "KT has stage fright, as I'm sure Mom told you. You know she's supposed to perform at our parents' benefit concert, too?"

"Yes."

"Is that enough time to help her overcome her fears?"

"If she wants to overcome them."

That was the rub, wasn't it? "Fair enough. I can get her to come see you. Do you have an office in the city?"

He handed her a card. "Downtown. Lara led me to believe it might be difficult to get Karma to come in to see me."

"My sister will do anything for me," she said, giving him an intent look as she slipped the card into her sports bra alongside Gwen's.

To his credit, his gaze didn't waver from her face. "You believe that," he said.

"I know that, because I'll do anything for her too."

He studied her intently, as though he could see into her. "I believe it. Bring her in tomorrow, at two."

Bijou held her hand out. "It's a date."

He took her hand and held it firm and steady in his. "I'm looking forward to it."

Heaven help her, she thought, feeling a shiver of pleasure from his touch, so was she.

Chapter Three

As Chance Nolan bent to stretch his hamstrings, he gave his buddy a stern look. "You better get ready to run. You've been eating a lot, and I don't want a porker on my hands."

His little pig, Ante Up, tossed its snout in the air.

"I know you're young, but if you don't start working out now, you're going to lose your figure. It's all in the genetics, my friend, and I've seen pictures of your mother."

He swore the pig rolled his eyes before trotting away to investigate the vast Carrington-Wright garden.

Chance rolled his eyes, too. If someone had told him one day his closest friend would be a farm animal, he'd have laughed—hard. When he won the pig in a poker game a couple months ago, he'd thought he'd give it away or sell it, but in the end he hadn't been able to. The little sucker was too endearing.

Part of the reason Chance remained in San Francisco was because of Ante Up. A pig wasn't meant to live on a boat. Ante Up had been a good sailor, all things considered, but Chance could tell the oinker was happier on terra firma.

Frankly, Chance was happier, too. After college, when all his friends had gone back home to establish their lives, he'd been at a loss over what to do. When he'd won the boat in a poker game, he'd decided it was a great idea to set sail. It wasn't as though he had a home to go back to.

It'd been the best decision he'd ever made. It'd been what he needed to distance himself from the past. At first, he'd been lonely, but he'd grown to enjoy the solitude. It made him look forward to pulling into port and connecting with people. He supported himself by playing poker whenever he needed to. He'd spent many a night on yachts of rich men, winning money and jewelry from them.

Now it was time for a new chapter.

He'd realized it as he'd set sail for California. It was time to give up the gypsy lifestyle and lay down roots. He'd begun yearning for things he hadn't wanted before. A family. A purpose. He couldn't be a poker player forever. At some point his luck would turn.

He'd known as soon as he'd arrived in San Francisco for his college buddy Scott's wedding that this was the place where he was going to stay. Scott's mom, Elise, had very sweetly encouraged him to stay with her while he looked for an apartment and employment.

Ironically, it was at Scott's wedding where Chance had met Roger Leif, the CEO of a finance company, Paragon International Group. The moment Leif had discovered Chance played poker, he was eager to discuss hiring him.

A lot of finance companies hired poker players as quantitative analysts. It was right up his alley — he had a business degree, and he understood numbers.

More than that, he was excited about the opportunity. Some people might see researching investments and developing trading strategies as dull, but it was all a game, just like poker, and Chance loved to play. The only difference was that a nine to five job would give him the flexibility to have a life, as well as the stability of a paycheck.

"Chance! There you are."

He stiffened, recognizing the voice. He turned around to see Tiffany Woods headed toward him, as if he'd conjured her with his thoughts.

What was she doing here? How did she get his address?

His résumé. Of course. He internally groaned, wishing he'd had another option, but as the headhunter in charge of hiring for Paragon, Tiffany Woods was the person standing between him and the job. He had to give her whatever she needed. Within reason, because he knew she wanted way more from him than he was comfortable with.

She walked carefully toward him on her tiptoes, probably so the spiked heels she wore didn't sink into the grass.

Ante Up snorted derisively and trotted away. Chance couldn't blame him; she looked ridiculous teetering across the lawn.

She smiled brilliantly as she reached him. "I'm glad I caught you before you left. I got your résumé."

Obviously. He smiled politely. "I hope Roger will be able to meet soon."

"I think we can arrange that." She gave him

a shark-like grin. "I'm sure we can find a way to help each other out."

As a poker player, he knew how to read people. When he looked at Tiffany Woods, he recognized the look in her eyes, and he was pretty sure she meant helping each other out of their clothes.

He might have been flattered under normal circumstances—she wasn't unattractive. Most of his friends would have loved to be preyed on by her. She was blond and petite and beautiful in the way expensive women were perfectly put together. He knew from past girlfriends that she probably took over an hour to do her makeup to make it look "natural" and that her shoes cost a fortune.

He'd never understood why women paid so much for shoes that they couldn't walk in—it defeated the purpose of footwear.

The problem here was that she stood in the way of his dream job. Nothing good could come from a fling with the woman who was the gatekeeper to the company he hoped to work for.

Which was why he couldn't just tell her to go away. So he said, "Thanks for taking the time to come over."

Ante Up made a derisive noise, clearly calling him a coward. But what was he supposed to do? He had to play his cards right.

"I was thinking of going to lunch." Tiffany flipped her hair back. "Want to join me? I can tell you more about Paragon. I know a great place that has an outdoor patio."

"Sorry. I'm about to take Ante Up for a run."

She barely gave the pig a glance. "Then maybe another time."

"Sure," he said noncommittally.

"Like tomorrow."

Chance started to say no, deciding that maybe it was a good idea to set the boundaries clearly, but then he saw a glimmer of something in her gaze that shocked him. Loneliness.

He understood loneliness — too well.

But he wanted to smack himself upside the head when he heard himself say, "I need to check my calendar. Why don't you text me?"

"I can do that." She reached out and caressed his arm. "Chance, I think this is a fantastic opportunity, and we're looking forward to seeing a lot more of you."

He subtly extricated himself from her clutches. "Well—"

The hedges to the left began to rustle. Ante Up snorted and waddled over to investigate as a long jean-covered leg appeared over the top of the high bush. The second leg slung over, followed by a surprisingly shapely ass. The woman dangled up high by her hands and then dropped into the yard with a billow of honey hair and a muffled "Oof."

Chance recognized her as Scott's best man, a childhood friend who lived next door. He'd met her at the wedding, but he couldn't remember her name. It was something strange.

Like he could judge.

And not like it mattered. The important thing was that she was here. It was like the universe was handing him a gift, and he never looked a gift horse in the mouth.

In this case, the universe was giving him a graceful way of letting Tiffany know he wasn't available without making her feel inadequate. Smiling, he turned to the blonde and said, "Tiffany, have you met my girlfriend?"

"What?" Tiffany's shocked gaze flew to the woman.

Who frowned at them as she stood up and brushed her butt off. "What are you doing here?" Scott's friend asked.

"Waiting for you." He strode to his new girl-friend, tugged her into his arms, and laid a big kiss on her.

Her hands came to his chest. He waited for her to push him away, or to slap him, or knee him in the nuts. All valid options and certainly all de-served.

It shocked him when instead she melted against him and wound her arms around his neck, pressing herself more fully against him.

His body woke up, at attention. Everything but the lush feel of her mouth on his and the long length of her against him faded away. He clutched her shirt and brought her closer, liking the way she hummed.

Because she let him, he slowed the kiss, deep-ening it. She was scorching and eager, and his only thought was that he didn't mind playing with fire.

Her breathing heavy, she disengaged from his

lips without moving an inch. Her half-lidded gaze went from his mouth to his eyes, and back to his mouth.

He pushed her hair out of her eyes. They were hazel, a complicated kaleidoscope of colors. "If I do that again, will you slap me?"

"I'll slap you if you don't," she said as she resumed kissing him.

Her T-shirt rose up, and he put his hand on the warm skin of her waist. She felt resilient and soft, and he couldn't help trailing his hand up her back, along her spine. He felt goosebumps raise on her skin and the low murmur of what he hoped was pleasure.

Something bumped his leg. He was going to ignore it when he felt a nip at his calf. "What the hell?" he exclaimed, glaring down.

Ante Up gave him a piggy grin, waving his snout up and down.

"Is that a pig?" Scott's gorgeous friend asked, still in his arms.

"Yeah." He looked around, relieved to see that Tiffany had left. Since there didn't seem to be a reason to kiss her any longer, except that he wanted to, he let her go. "Thanks for helping me out. I couldn't get rid of her."

"The pig?"

"Tiffany Woods. She's the main headhunter at a firm I'm interviewing with."

"I thought she looked like a cannibal."

"Not that sort of headhunter, though I wouldn't be surprised if I heard rumors of discarded bodies."

The woman snapped her fingers. "I know where I've seen you. You're a friend of Scott's. You were here for the spectacle."

"Spectacle?"

"Or wedding." She waved her hand back and forth. "To-may-to, to-mah-to."

He liked her. Grinning, he held out his hand. "Chance Nolan. You live next door."

She shrugged as she shook his hand. "It's a burden I carry."

He held it in his, reluctant to let it go. "First tell me your name, then tell me why you climbed over the bushes."

She sighed. "Neither one is a pretty story."

"Name first."

"KT."

"The only time people go by their initials is when they have hideous names."

"Exactly."

"What's yours?"

"Like hell I'm giving you ammunition like that." She crossed her arms and frowned at him.

"I can guess."

Sighing again, she shook her head. "No, you really couldn't."

"Katunia." At her raised brow, he continued. "Keisha. Kayla. Kevin. Kevlar."

"You had to go to bullet-proof material?"

He shrugged. "You seem tough."

She snorted.

Ante Up snorted, too.

KT reached down and scratched the pig behind his ears. Chance swore the porker's eyes rolled back in pleasure. "I must be speaking his language," she said.

Or else it just confirmed that his pig was as smart as Chance believed. "Okay, you won't tell me your name, so tell me why you were climbing into the Carrington-Wright yard."

"That's because my name is lame, and I hopped

the fence to get away from my mom. She keeps trying to set me up with men."

"You don't like men?"

"I don't like the men she brings home for me. I like men fine." She stared at his lips.

He felt the power of that stare in places she wasn't overtly checking out.

KT cleared her throat. "Well, I should go. Good luck with Tiffany. Looks like you'll need it."

"Wait." He grabbed her hand before she got away. He didn't need luck when he had KT. "Be my girlfriend."

"Excuse me?"

He hadn't planned it out but now it seemed like a brilliant idea. "Pretend to be my girlfriend, just until I get the job and Tiffany is no longer an issue. I want the job, but if she harbors romantic delusions, it's going to be tricky."

She smirked. "It's hard being hot, isn't it, hot shot?"

"I'm giving you a solution to both our problems and you're mocking me?"

"I'm impossible." She shrugged. "And it's only a temporary solution."

"I'll sweeten the pot," he said.

"How?"

"You'll get to kiss me any time," he said impulsively, hoping it was as tempting to her as it was to him.

Her eyes zeroed in on his lips again. "And, what? Go on pretend dates?"

"Yes. It'll get your mom off your back."

"True. And will we pretend kiss?"

"I'm not sure there'll be any pretending there." He lowered his lips to hers, because he couldn't help it.

"I feel like I'm signing away my soul," she whispered against his mouth.

"Don't worry, I'll keep it safe for you." He slid his hand under her shirt again. "We should do something to mark the beginning of a beautiful relationship."

"Save it for when we have an audience, Bogart." She patted his chest and stepped away.

"Want my number?" he asked, willing her to say yes.

Rolling her eyes, she got her phone out. "Give it to me."

Reciting it slowly, he watched her save it, her brow furrowed in concentration. She gave him an undecipherable look before she left him. He watched her lovely ass sway as she sashayed into Elise's house, wondering where she was going and when he'd get to kiss her again.

Chapter Four

*H*ER MUSIC WAS sacred.

Even when KT wrote pop songs for Jamila, she'd taken her music seriously. She had focus, and no one interrupted her for threat of loss of life.

But today as she began to play her concerto, her mind wandered. Instead of rewriting the end of the middle section, which still wasn't quite right, she thought about Chance.

She thought about kissing Chance.

She wasn't a stranger to kisses. She may have liked her privacy, but she wasn't a prude. Her first kiss had been at a party in Mick Jagger's home. She'd been ten, and the nephew of some other guest had cornered her behind a zebra-print curtain.

Chance kissed much better than that boy.

Her music took a turn, infused with passion borrowed from the memory of Chance's lips on hers. Soft and lingering at first, a hushed focus that built into the promise of erotic completion.

She played faster, humming along, her fingers almost stumbling over themselves as her music fell into place. The piano sang with unrestrained desire, a need that thundered through her, too.

It ended on a sudden, startling note. KT sat there, breathing hard, her heart pounding. And then she grabbed her pencil and began scribbling the notes, replaying what her fingers had done in her head, and she scrambled to get it all down.

The front door opened.

She turned around to glare at whoever entered. "What the hell? I'm working."

Her mom stood in the doorway, looking every bit the rock diva in torn jeans and a vintage Beatles T-shirt tied at the waist. She had bracelets up her arms, rings on her fingers and toes, and big hoop earrings. Her hair streamed down her back. It should have looked ridiculous on a woman her age but on Lara Taylor, it was perfect. KT felt the combination of love, admiration, and envy she always felt for her mother.

Until Lara spoke. "Karma, are you a lesbian?"

KT sputtered incoherently. "Mom."

Her mom closed the door and stepped into the

cottage. "There's nothing wrong with it, sweeting. In my day, I kissed a girl or two myself."

"Mother."

"I don't know what you expect me to think." She trailed her fingers on the piano keys before resting her elbow on the top and propping her chin up. "You clearly aren't interested in seeing men."

That wasn't entirely true. She was very interested in seeing Chance again—in public or private.

She thought about their deal. It wasn't as much a deal as it was insanity. Pretend to date? It couldn't work.

Except maybe . . . Because if he could kiss her that convincingly before they had a deal, just think of how he'd kiss now that they had an agreement.

She looked at her mom. She wasn't sure she could lie to her, no matter how crazy the woman was driving her.

Lara returned her gaze pleasantly. "Have you thought about what you're going to wear on stage when you perform, Karma?"

"I'm seeing someone, Mom," she blurted.

Her mom just stared. "I think I need to get my

hearing checked, because I thought I just heard you say you're seeing someone."

Her face flushed hot. It wouldn't be a lie if she and Chance actually did see each other a few times. It wasn't like she said she was going to have his babies or anything. They'd "go out" a few times and then she'd break up with him. Or vice versa. Whatever. "You didn't hear wrong."

"A man?"

"No, a vibrator." She rolled her eyes. "Of course, a man, Mom. Geez."

Lara shrugged. "It never hurts to ask for clarification. What's his name?"

"Chance Nolan."

"Oh, I like it." Her eyes became dreamy. "He sounds yummy. Does he have good hands?"

KT covered her eyes. "Please don't go there, Mother."

"He must, if you're blushing that way." Her mother arched a brow at her. "It's not how much they've got that counts, Karma. It's how they use it. Take your father, for instance."

"I'd really rather not." She'd covered the wrong body part. She clenched her palms over her ears instead of her eyes.

Lara pulled KT's hands away. "There's nothing to be ashamed about, Karma. You know your father and I are sexual beings."

Why couldn't she have normal parents, who didn't talk about sex and ignored her?

"When is Chance coming over?" Lara asked.

"Never," she murmured.

"Karma."

That motherly tone with faint disapproval got her every time. She sighed. "I'll ask him."

Lara clapped her hands. "Excellent. Have him come over this afternoon."

Dread pooled in her stomach. "I don't know if he's free this afternoon."

"He'll be free." She kissed KT's forehead, brushing back her bangs. "I'm so happy you finally met someone you're interested in. I only want you to be as happy as your father and I are."

She wilted. Oh, the guilt. "I know. It's just I'm different than you guys."

"Of course you're your own person, Karma, but I think you underestimate who you are."

"Who am I?"

"I think you're going to find out over the next few weeks, before the concert." Her mother smiled mysteriously.

She watched her mother walk away, not feeling reassured at all. She was still staring at the door when it reopened and her sister breezed in.

KT frowned. "What is this? Grand Central?"

"Do you know Gwen?" Bijou asked, ignoring the sarcasm. "She owns the gourd art store on Sacramento."

"What the heck is gourd art?"

Bijou held up her hand. "Before you disparage her pumpkins, you should see them. Her work is amazing."

"If you say so."

Her sister rolled her eyes. "Forget the gourds."

"You're the one who brought them up."

"As a frame of reference, not as the main note. Gwen has a charity for kids in the Mission, and she's looking for a music teacher for a particular kid who apparently has skills but not the money to take classes. She's supposed to be an idiot savant, like you."

"Don't call me names," KT joked halfheartedly.

Bijou smacked a business card on the top of the piano. "Call Gwen and set up teaching this kid."

She said the obvious. "I'm not a teacher."

"If you want to convince Mom you have a higher calling than strutting on a stage, then you better become one right away."

Actually, it was a good idea. Her mom couldn't complain if she thought KT was meant to be an instructor. Her parents held teachers in the highest regard. She could sell it as her way of giving back. "That's actually smart, Bijou."

Her sister rolled her eyes. "Gee, thanks, KT."

She ignored the sarcasm and thought out loud. "That, combined with the fact that I'm dating someone, should satisfy Mom."

"You're dating someone? Someone real?"

"Bijou."

Her sister shrugged. "Can you blame me for asking? Who is he?"

"His name is Chance Nolan. I met him at Scott's wedding." Which was true, if not completely accurate.

Bijou gaped at her and then burst out laughing.

"Chance and Karma! How perfect is that? If you have kids, you have to name them Faith and Hope."

She frowned, finding it way too easy to imagine having kids with Chance. "We just met."

"Karma and Chance, sitting in a tree . . ." Bijou lifted an eyebrow suggestively as she sashayed her skinny ass out.

She was not going to think about having babies with Chance. But Bijou was right about one thing, teaching music would go a long way toward satisfying their mom. Damn it. Maybe she could teach this kid without playing for her. If the kid really was a musical genius, she'd only need a few pointers.

KT gripped her head. Just days ago she was happy and uninterrupted in her own little world. Now everyone was harassing her.

Except Chance.

She got her phone out of her back pocket and called the number he gave her before she could talk herself out of it.

He answered on the second ring. "I was thinking about you right now."

His voice was low and husky, a sexy rasp in her ear — an auditory caress no less powerful than the feel of his hands on her skin the day before. "Did I have clothes on?"

"Do you need to ask?"

Was it stuffy in here? She fanned herself. "I didn't call to talk about your fantasies."

"Too bad."

Ignoring the fact that he actually sounded remorseful, she said, "You've received a royal summons."

"From?"

"My parents. Well, really my mom. Today I found out that she thinks I'm really a lesbian. I'm not sure she believes you exist."

"What time should I come over?"

"Like around four?"

"I'll be there."

He sounded calm and reassuring, like he had her back, and her heart did something weird. She put a hand on her chest, wondering if she could fit in a visit to the doctor before four and still wash her hair.

**KT strode to the entryway to the living room and peeked down the hall. No sign of Chance yet. She checked the time. 3:56. Still early.

Damn it.

Walking across the room, she looked out the window. She'd never introduced anyone new to her parents. Usually it was the other way around, with Lara shoving men at her. When he got here, should she kiss him hello? Was that too much in front of parents?

"Really, Karma, you're starting to make me nervous," her mother said from where she sat curled up on the couch flipping through a magazine. "You have me thinking that this Chance is an ogre or something."

Her dad looked up from the game he was playing on his iPhone. "Karma wouldn't date an ogre, would you, sweetie? She has better taste than that."

"How would we know, my love?" Lara looked at her husband fondly. "She's never brought home anyone before."

Her dad resettled his crooked glasses on his nose. "What about that unwashed man who smelled like thrift store?"

"That was Bijou, my love."

"Ah."

Oh geez. KT put a hand to her forehead, wondering if it was too late to call off Chance, because after meeting her parents he was sure to change his mind about pretend-dating her. But before she could do anything, the Addams Family doorbell sounded.

KT headed off Nellie, their housekeeper, at the door. "I got this."

"Okay, Miss Karma." Nellie stayed where she was in the hallway, waiting for the door to open.

KT sighed. Nellie had been their housekeeper since before she was born and was pretty much part of the family. She knew better than to try to shoo her away.

Taking a deep breath, she flung open the door.

Chance stood there, his hair rumpled and slight scruff shadowing his face. He wore slacks, shiny shoes, and a dress shirt open at the collar under a sports coat. He should have looked like a business douchebag, but he just looked really hot. She felt herself flush as she imagined ripping the buttons off the shirt and baring his chest.

Swallowing her lust, she said, "You clean up."

"So do you." He looked her over appreciatively.

"I'm only wearing jeans." Though she had found time to wash her hair. It fell down her back in clean waves, so she had that going for her.

"I like you in jeans." He gripped her waist and gave her a light kiss on the lips.

She blinked, not startled by the casual intimacy but by how right it felt.

He must have seen her surprise, because he whispered, "We have an audience. I thought I'd sell it."

Nellie—right. She tried not to feel disappointed as she pulled him inside. "Where's the pig?"

"I thought you'd want to introduce Ante Up to your parents next time. He takes some adjusting to."

"Good thinking. My mom might get it in her head that she wants a piglet of her own and then my dad would hate you."

"Whew. Disaster narrowly averted." He slid his arm around her.

Nellie didn't wait for KT to introduce her. She strode right up to Chance and stuck her hand out. "I'm Nellie Ramsey, the Taylors' housekeeper."

"Chance Nolan." He shook her hand, flashing her a charming smile.

Nellie used his hand to yank him down to her. "I've known Karma since she was born, so you better be on your best behavior with her."

"Yes, ma'am," he said quickly. KT gave him props for the lack of sarcasm.

Nellie stared at him with her laser ray vision, nodding when she decided he was sincere. She let go of his hand and smiled at him. "You'll do nicely. The duo is in the living room. I'll bring refreshments in a moment. I hope you're hungry."

"Starving," he claimed.

Nellie beamed. "Good. You children go ahead now."

"Are you really starving?" KT asked softly as Nellie puttered toward the kitchen.

"Let's just say I know well enough to eat whatever she puts in front of me." He took her hand. "Lead the way, Karma."

KT groaned. "Please don't. And please don't say we can name our child Kismet."

"It never crossed my mind."

She glanced at him. "Liar."

He grinned. "What did Nellie mean by 'the duo'?"

"I didn't tell you about my parents, did I?" she said with a wince.

"They can't be that bad."

"Bad? No." Just the biggest rock stars in the world, next to the Beatles and U2. How did you tell a potential boyfriend that?

"Let me be surprised," he said, letting her off the hook. He kissed her quickly. "It'll be fine, KT. This is pretend, remember?"

Right. Nodding, she led him to the living room. She tried to imagine what his first impression of her parents would be. Of course, he'd recognize who they were—natives from the darkest parts of Papua New Guinea knew Anson and Lara. But the reality of them was different altogether.

Her dad was still playing on his phone, but her mother had set aside her magazine and was impatiently waiting. When they walked in, the smile on her face turned to a frown. "Karma, he's a suit! I raised you better than that."

Before KT could do anything, like die of mortification, Chance stepped forward, took off his coat, and tossed it on a chair to the side as he extended his hand to her mom. "Actually, I'm a bum posing as a suit. I was looking at an apartment to lease today and thought they'd be more likely to rent to someone who looked like he showered occasionally."

"Oh." Her mother beamed, her hands outstretched. "In that case, welcome, Chance. I'm Lara."

"I see that." He kissed her mom's uplifted cheek. "I can see where KT got her beauty from. Your TV appearances don't do you justice."

"Aren't you a dear?" Still holding his hand, she led him to the couch. "Come sit with me, Chance. Anson, my love, Karma's beau is here."

Her dad lifted his head from his game and smiled happily. "I'm afraid I have an Angry Birds addiction."

Chance grinned as he rolled up his sleeves. "I hear they have a twelve-step program for it now."

Lara smiled at her husband fondly as she curled back onto the couch. "He's entitled to a vice or two. Karma, stop looming and come join us."

KT sighed as she slouched onto an oversized chair across from her mom and Chance. This was going to be a long afternoon.

"So, Chance"—Lara focused her bright gaze on Chance—"how strong is your sex drive?"

Groaning, KT smacked a hand over her eyes. "Seriously, Mother? That's where you're going to start the interrogation?"

"Life starts with sex, Karma. And, really, your father and I would love to have grandchildren before we're infirm."

Chance chuckled. "You still have decades before that'll be a concern."

"You're so sweet." Lara patted his arm. "Your mother raised you right. Where do your parents live?"

His face shuttered, devoid of all emotion. "My family died in an accident when I was eighteen."

Blinking, KT sat up. She hadn't known. Logically, she knew there was no way that she could have—they'd only just met—but it seemed like something even a pretend girlfriend would know.

Her mom looked stricken. She took his hand, squeezing it. "Oh, you poor dear boy. I'm so sorry."

"It was a long time ago," he said in the same guarded voice.

KT willed him to look at her, so she could see if he was okay, but he avoided eye contact. She cleared her throat. "Mom, Chance has a little pig."

Her mother shot her a grateful smile. "Do you, Chance? How peculiar."

He also shot KT a look, but she couldn't tell what it meant. Before she could decipher it, he faced Lara and said, "His name is Ante Up. I won him in a poker game."

"You play poker?" her dad asked suddenly, popping his head out of his game. "Online?"

"Not online. Mostly unorganized games." Chance leaned forward, elbows on his knees and hands steepled. "Until I came to San Francisco, I lived in the Caribbean on my boat."

"You're an adventurer," Lara said enthusiastically. Then she looked lovingly at Anson. "My love, do you remember the time we chartered the boat in Greece?"

Her dad smiled fondly. "I remember you went topless every day and how we made love like —"

"Okay!" KT jumped up. "Well, we have to go now."

Her parents blinked at her, confused. Chance just looked entertained.

"But, sweeting," her mom protested, "Nellie hasn't even brought the scones yet. I had her make the citrus ones you love."

The citrus scones. She paused, tempted, but then she imagined what else her parents would tell Chance and pictured him running off, screaming, which was an unhappy image. So she said, "We have plans for, um, dinner."

Her mother glanced at the delicate Rolex on her wrist. "It's just after four, Karma."

"I didn't have lunch." She took Chance's hand, ignoring the amused look on his face.

She expected her mom to ask more questions, but the woman just smiled peacefully and said, "Have fun, children. Chance, we'll have to have you over for dinner. You haven't met Bijou yet."

"Anytime." He shook Anson's hand and picked up his jacket as Karma dragged him away.

"I have questions," he said softly, close to her ear as she marched him out of the house.

"Of course you do."

"Who's Bijou?"

"My sister." She winced, thinking about him meeting her. Men liked Bijou. The thought of Chance preferring her made KT pout. "She's the pretty one."

"I doubt that." His thumb caressed her hand. "Second question. Am I missing out on the scones?"

"Nellie's citrus scones are like a taste of heaven," she said reverently.

"Damn." He stopped, pulling her into him. "You're going to have to make it up to me."

She swallowed at the hungry look in his eyes. "You don't mean food, do you?"

"No, I don't." He traced a finger across her lower lip. "You protected me back there."

She hadn't been able to bear the blank look that, she was positive, covered up a sadness too deep for words. But she didn't want to seem like a sap, so she shrugged. "I got you into the situation. It was the least I could do."

He studied her. "You've got an awful poker face."

"Like hell." She frowned. "I'm great at poker."

"Then we should play sometime," he said in a husky voice that told her exactly how high the stakes would be.

Something in her belly tightened. She wanted to flirt back at him, but she could only nod.

"Good." He lowered his head and kissed her, slowly and delicately, like she was to be savored. Like she was as delicious as Nellie's scones.

She melted against him, unable to help herself and not really caring. Against his lips, she murmured, "There's no one watching here."

"I know." He kissed her again as if punctuating that statement. Then he lifted her chin and said, "Where are we going?"

"I don't care." As long as she was with him. "I just had to get you out of there before my mom handed you a box of condoms."

"Would she have done that?"

"Hell yes."

He laughed. "She's amazing. I love them."

A warm feeling spread through her. Not wanting to analyze it, she squeezed his hand. "Come on. There's a café a few blocks away that has great pastries."

"Citrus scones?"

"No, but their croissants are to die for."

"Lead the way." He grinned. "I'm yours to command."

She looked at him. "Really?"

The amusement in his expression turned hot and feral. "Keep staring at me like that and you'll find out."

She swallowed thickly, her chest tight with excitement, because for the first time ever, she was tempted. Really, really tempted.

Chapter Five

CHANCE COULDN'T THINK of anything better than walking hand in hand with KT. Well—actually he could, and it involved whipped cream and a whole lot of naked flesh.

Meeting a woman's parents had always served like birth control in the past, but this time it'd been different. This time, he sat in that amazingly down-to-earth living room and wanted to belong to that family, as kooky as they were.

As if knowing the direction of his thoughts, KT turned to him and said, "I didn't know your parents had died. I'm sorry."

Like always when someone brought it up, he shut down. "You play the hand you're dealt. It was a long time ago."

"It doesn't matter." KT stopped, making him face her. Putting her hand on his chest right over his heart, she gave him that clear, no-nonsense gaze. "You obviously loved them. That never goes away."

He was surprised to hear himself say, "My two brothers were in the car, too. They were on their way home from a family dinner. I was supposed to be there, but I caught a cold and didn't go home from my prep school that weekend."

She swallowed audibly. "You had two brothers?"

"Older." He could still feel the way they used to scrub his head and mess up his hair. "My parents named me Chance, because they wanted a daughter and took a chance on their third child."

Her hand fisted on his shirt. "I can't even imagine. My mother drives me crazy, but the thought of losing her, or Dad, or Bijou . . ."

"Don't think about it," he said, hating the hoarseness in his voice. "Tell her you love her every day, even when you want to run away from her."

She nodded, giving him the gentlest kiss. "Okay."

He exhaled loudly, running a hand through his hair. "I should be over it. It was over a decade ago."

"They were your parents." She started walking again, more slowly this time, obviously thinking. "And it sounds like you were close to your brothers."

"They were the ones who taught me how to

play poker." He smiled, remembering how they used to let him stay up with them and play even though they were so much older in high school, and he was a lowly sixth grader. "They didn't know it, but they saved my life by teaching me to play. My parents had just enough life insurance to pay off their debts, and even selling the house wasn't enough to pay for four years at Harvard. I paid my way through school by playing. It's how I got the boat."

"So you set sail." She nodded. "And you got a friend."

"He's some pig." Chance squeezed her hand when she chuckled. Something lightened in his chest at the sound, and he felt a wave of appreciation so strong he wanted to grab her up and squeeze her. But that'd only scare her, so instead he looked at her and said, "Thank you."

Her wide brow furrowed. "For what?"

"For being great." He tugged her toward him and ran his hand down her long hair. "You're the best pretend girlfriend I've ever had."

"I try."

"You should be rewarded."

She lit up. "Unlimited pretend kisses?"

"The unlimited real kisses are already yours." He gave her a quick one, wishing they were somewhere more private. "I was thinking something different."

"Like?"

His gaze caught on a sign that read Fine Lingerie. "There."

KT's brow wrinkled, but she reluctantly followed his lead. "Is this a reward for me or you?"

"Both."

She pursed her lips. "That sounded like a promise."

"It was," he assured her as he pulled her into the store called Romantic Notions.

A bell peeled softly as they entered, and a dark-haired lady looked up from where she was hanging bras. She smiled invitingly at the two of them. "I was thinking of closing, but I realize I stayed open just for you two."

KT's face looked relieved. "If you're closing —"

"Honey, he doesn't look like he's going to let you out of here so easily." The woman winked. "Indulge him. It looks like it'll be worth it in the end."

"Trust her," Chance said with a raised brow.

KT rolled her eyes, but there was a smile hovering at the edge of her lips.

"My name is Olivia," the woman said. "Take a look around while I go change this guy. When you're ready for help let me know."

Chance and KT looked down at the floor where there was a happy squeal of a toddler. He had light hair but his mother's dark eyes, and he laughed when his mother scooped him up and airplaned him over her head.

Rubbing his hands together, Chance looked around the store. "I feel like a kid in a candy store."

KT rolled her eyes. "Men are so predictable."

"I'm not predictable, babe." He walked over to a white bra made of the sheerest lace he'd ever seen. Just the thought of seeing her in it, her nipples peeking darkly from the lace, got him going. "I like this."

"Seriously?" She looked at it skeptically. "It's kind of plain, isn't it?"

"It's what's inside that counts, not the packaging." He held it out. "What size are you?"

She shrugged, her cheeks flushing.

"You don't know." He stared, intrigued. "You don't wear bras, do you?"

She glared at him. "You wear one and tell me they aren't modern torture devices."

He walked over to her, taking her in his arms and trailing his hands up her spine. Instead of an elastic band anywhere, he felt the supple muscles of her back. He felt a surge of need—need to feel her in front, need to lift her shirt up and see the naked evidence for himself. "The thought that you're naked under this shirt is driving me crazy."

"Everyone's naked under their clothes." She shrugged at the look he gave her. "Well, it's true."

Olivia came out from the back carrying the little boy, who squirmed until she let him down. She nodded at the bra in his hand. "That piece is beautiful on. You want to try it on?"

"She does," Chance said before KT could say anything. "The underwear, too."

Olivia winked at him and faced KT. "Don't worry, honey. I specialize in making this painless. Go through the curtain, and I'll be back in a second."

KT trudged off like she was on her way to the electric chair.

Grinning, Olivia touched his arm. "I'll do my part and then you do yours, and we'll convert her to a lingerie girl yet."

Chance smiled. "I'd like to see that."

"I know you would." She winked at him and went behind the curtain. "Don't let Parker pull down the displays. I'll be right back."

He looked down at the boy, who'd somehow snuck up and sat looking up at him. Chance knelt down and pointed to the truck in the kid's hand. "Truck?"

The kid lit up. "Vroom!" he said enthusiastically.

When KT and Olivia came out of the back, he was lying on the floor letting the boy drive the truck all over his body, occasionally lurching like he was an earthquake just to hear the boy laugh.

"This is interesting," KT said with a lift of her brow.

"I was doing as I was told." He ran a hand over the kid's head and got up. "How was it?"

KT shrugged. "Okay."

"It looked awesome on her," Olivia assured him. "She's getting it."

"I'm getting it for her." He pulled out his wallet at he met them at the counter.

"No." KT put a hand on his to stall him. "I'll buy it."

He leaned in so his lips were against her ear, and he whispered, "I'm buying it. It's my way of giving you a handicap when we play strip poker."

"You think I need an advantage?"

"That, too." He kissed her and then handed his card to Olivia.

"Oh boy," Olivia said. "The game is on."

Chapter Six

*B*IJOU STOOD ON a raised platform in the middle of her best friend's loft, staring at the reflection of herself in a wedding dress in the three-way mirror in front of her. Filling the living space that doubled as a showroom, there were mannequins, all wearing wedding dresses designed by Rosalind, like headless bridal sentries.

It was surreal.

Bijou touched the lace cap sleeve of the dress Rosalind had made her try on. It was wispy, like gossamer petals. The lower half of the gown draped in longer layers of the same fairy material.

She started to fidget, but then stopped when she remembered Rosalind's not-so-veiled threats about unraveling the loose stitches. Bijou felt— odd. She'd never had cause to try on a wedding dress before. She always expected to get married, just not until she got her career established. She'd never even imagined it.

But now, standing in some other woman's dress, she couldn't help picturing herself walking down the aisle. In a perfect world, her sister would sing a song Bijou had written specially for the day, and her dad would walk her to meet her beloved, who'd wait for her with an expression of awe and adoration.

For some reason, her imaginary groom looked just like Will Shaw, which was absolutely ridiculous, because he was so her type. There's no way was she going to marry someone she was attracted to.

"Crazy," she muttered, shaking her head.

"What's crazy?" Rosalind asked, re-entering her loft's large living area, which doubled as a showroom. She slipped a pincushion around her wrist and frowned as she fiddled with the neckline.

"Using me to fit this dress," she improvised, not wanting to open that can of worms. Rosalind had known her too long and too well. They'd met each other at boarding school. Rosalind had been there on forbearance, because her father had lost most of his fortune and couldn't afford the steep tuition. She and Bijou used to joke that they'd been made roommates because they were both pariahs. Bijou, the gauche daughter of American rock stars, and Rosalind, the impoverished daughter of an earl. It'd been instant kinship that had lasted years. "Isn't it bad luck for me to wear the bride's dress?"

Rosalind shook her head as she pinned the bodice. "That's an old wives' tale. You're the same size as she is, only taller, and I'd much rather have you here than her. But if it makes you feel any better, this wedding is already doomed to fail. In which case, it's important that the bride at least looks fabulous so I get the repeat business."

Bijou grinned. "You're heartless."

"I'm a businesswoman at heart. A quarter turn, love."

She glanced at her watch. "How much longer?"

"Do you have someplace to be?" her friend asked as she rearranged the drape of the train.

"Yes." KT's appointment with Will Shaw. Though KT didn't know about it, so Bijou had to wrangle her.

Rosalind paused and looked up at her suspiciously. "Where?"

"None of your business."

Rosalind quirked her eyebrow. "Maybe I'll be designing a dress for you sooner than expected."

"You can't seriously think that, considering my past."

"Darling, Brice was a wanker. You can't judge all men by him."

"I'm not," she lied.

"Are you seriously going to try to lie to me?"

Bijou sighed. "It's complicated."

"As it always is with you, love." Rosalind smiled at her impishly. "Following you and your family is better than watching Downton Abbey."

"If only you'd seen the current episode, where Mom and KT have a showdown."

"Really." Her friend sat back on her heels. "Do tell."

"It'd require several hours and at least one bottle of wine."

"Tomorrow night, then." She stood up. "Go ahead and get dressed. Be careful not to dislodge the pins."

"As if I don't know the routine." She'd been

Rosalind's live mannequin since they were fourteen and Rosalind had decided that one day she was going to become a world famous wedding dress designer. She was on her way, too.

Bijou stepped off the platform carefully, admiring her reflection one more time. "Your dresses really are magic."

"It is lovely, isn't it? It's a shame this marriage is doomed."

Bijou shifted her attention to her friend. "Why are you so sure of that?"

"She's getting married for the wedding and all it entails." She reached out to reset the neckline. "It's not about her relationship. I almost didn't design the dress, but her mother looked so hopeful, I felt bad for her."

"Maybe because of your own mom?" Bijou asked with a raised brow.

Rosalind smiled. "We're all victims of our upbringing, but since when did you take up psychoanalysis?"

Since she'd met Will Shaw.

Fortunately, she didn't have to answer because Rosalind pushed her toward the dressing room elegantly screened off to the side. "Go. I'll make us tea."

"You're so British," Bijou teased, stepping behind the screen.

"Perhaps because I was born and raised there."

"No kidding, Lady Rosalind. Thanks, but I really have to go." She changed quickly, but carefully. Knowing better than to drape the dress on the chair in the dressing area, she brought it out and handed it to Rosalind.

Her friend took it to her sewing station, carefully hanging it. "Are you sure you can't stay? It's been an age since we've chatted. I miss you. I saw you more when you were in LA."

"I've been busy practicing for the concert." She picked up her purse. "I need my performance to be flawless."

"Flawless doesn't exist, love," Rosalind said.

"It has to." She gave her friend a one-armed hug. "Let's have lunch tomorrow."

"The American Grilled Cheese Kitchen?"

"Of course." Grinning, she waved over her shoulder as she let herself out of the loft. The second she was outside, she pulled out her phone and called KT. "We have an appointment with a therapist in half an hour."

"For what? Because our parents are insane?"

"No, to get you ready for stage, just in case your plan doesn't work."

"It's going to work."

Bijou sighed, picturing the stubborn set to her sister's lips. Their dad got the same look when he dug his heels in. "It can't hurt to just try Will. He's a good guy and nice to talk to."

"Then you go talk to him. I have someplace to be."

"Where?" she asked with disbelief.

"Your friend Gwen's foundation."

"You're going?"

"You don't have to sound so surprised," KT grumbled.

"I can't help it." But she was also pleased because this would be good for her sister. "What if I make an appointment for you with Will tomorrow?"

"I have a date."

Bijou tripped. "A date?"

"You don't have to sound like the world is

ending," her sister said indignantly. "I told you I was seeing someone."

"Yeah, but I didn't think you were serious."

"I'm here. I have to go. Bye."

"Wait—"

But KT had already hung up.

Bijou tapped the phone to her lips. She could call Will to tell him KT was a no-show, but it was so last minute. She should tell him in person.

KT would have said bullshit to that excuse.

Whatever—KT wasn't here. Bijou headed to Will's office, a feeling of anticipation fluttering in her belly, just like right before she stepped out on stage.

His office was downtown in an old building off Pine. She expected his office itself to be sparse and modern, but it was surprisingly colorful and warm. There was an Indian rug on the floor in the waiting room and a bright, inviting couch. The walls were lined with pictures of jazz musicians, all signed.

Interesting. Since there was no receptionist, Bijou sat down and waited, knowing instinctively that he'd come get her when he was ready.

On the hour, Will opened the door and smiled at her. "Bijou, it's good to see you."

Her heart leapt in her throat at the sight of him. He looked pretty much like he had the other day, only better. More masculine in the dress shirt with the sleeves rolled up and the open collar showing off his leather necklace.

In a former life she'd have been all over him, but in this one she knew better. It'd be really inconvenient to start something with another playboy right before getting her life back on track.

Okay—she had no idea if he really was a playboy, but what were the chances he wasn't? He wore a leather necklace—pretty much a playboy's tramp stamp.

She wouldn't be weak, and she wouldn't let her hormones get the better of her again. So she stood up with all the hauteur in her body, not wanting to let on how much the sight of him affected her. "Hello, Will Shaw," she said calmly, as if he wasn't delicious.

Looking behind her, he asked, "Where's Karma?"

"She goes by KT, and she couldn't make it."

She walked into his office and went directly to the couch, perching on the edge instead of lying down on it. She wasn't the patient here.

Will pulled a chair closer and sat across from her. "You could have called instead of coming all this way to tell me your sister couldn't make it."

"I didn't want to stand you up on such short notice."

"You care about that?"

"Don't get any ideas in your head. In a former life, I'd have been all over you, but I know better now."

An amused spark lit his face. "And why is that?"

"Are you shrinking me?" She narrowed her gaze. "I'm not the patient here, my sister is."

"But you're here and she's not."

"Don't try to be clever."

"Sorry." He covered his mouth with his steepled hands.

"I still see the edges of your smile."

"You caught me." He rubbed his palms on his thighs, his smile in full bloom. "What would you like to talk about?"

Everything. Her stalled career. The fact that

she hadn't been able to write a song in forever. Her miserable love life. The lightness she felt when she knew she'd see Will.

And nothing. She lived out loud, but in her core she was a private person. She knew she had walls, but they were there for a reason. Look what happened with Brice — she let him scale the walls and he stabbed her in the back.

The problem was that she already trusted Will. What was up with that? She barely knew him.

Knowing he was waiting, she decided to ask him something innocuous about KT, but what came out of her mouth was, "Have you ever had your heart broken?"

"Haven't we all?"

She pointed at him. "Don't play the therapist card here. I want to know about you."

He gazed at her silently. She didn't think he was going to answer but then he said, "Fair enough. Barbie Crenshaw. I met her sophomore year of college."

"Barbie?" Bijou couldn't hold back her snicker.

"Short for Barbara."

"Shouldn't that have been a clue? Never date

a woman named after a plastic doll."

"She was as far from the Barbie archetype as they come."

"But she broke your heart?"

"She was the one who got away." A faint smile curved his lips.

She hated Barbie.

"Who was yours?" he asked.

"My what?" She batted her lashes as if she were clueless.

"Don't play games with me, Bijou. You know what I meant."

Exhaling, she dropped the act. "Brice Bryland."

Will frowned. "The rock star?"

Only because of her song, the backstabbing fink. "Why do you sound so incredulous? I'm surrounded by rock stars just by virtue of who I was born."

"Tell me about him."

"No." She crossed her arms. "He's an ass."

Will's expression became an impartial mask. "Apparently you still have unresolved issues where he's concerned."

"The only unresolved issue I have is that his balls are still intact."

"Want to talk about it?"

"No."

"I don't understand, Bijou. You're here, but you don't want to discuss your past." He leaned his elbows on his knees. "What are you trying to accomplish? You obviously have a motive."

"I want KT to feel comfortable enough to go on stage."

"And?"

"That's it."

"I think your motives are more personal than that."

She laughed mirthlessly as she stood up. "It doesn't get more personal than that because if KT doesn't perform, I don't either."

He stood, too, and walked her to the door. "I don't know about that. I have a feeling you'll do what you set your mind to, regardless of anyone else."

She turned around, but the words on her tongue fled when she realized how close he was. She only had to lean a little to touch her lips to his.

Which would have been crazy. She stepped

back, her spine hitting the door post. "I'll bring KT next time. Same time, same place?"

"If you want."

"I do." Her cheeks flushed, remembering saying those words to him in her wedding dream, but she hurried out before he could wonder about her guilty thoughts.

Chapter Seven

IT TOOK KT twice as long to find the foundation as it should have, mostly because she got turned around on Valencia once she got off the bus. By the time she arrived there, she was twenty minutes late.

She pushed open the door to the Purple Elephant, wanting to go home and forget about all this, but she couldn't. It killed her to see the resigned look on her sister's face, like Bijou expected her to let her down. She couldn't let Bijou down but performing was even less an option. She'd make her plan work.

"KT?" a woman asked.

She turned to see a slight woman. She had curly hair streaked with orange pulled back into an elaborate braid-ponytail. She wore a striped top and paisley skirt in reds and purples and greens, and she somehow made the outfit look fashionable. Despite the cacophony of colors,

the most striking thing about her was her bright smile.

"You look like Bijou," the artist said, linking her arm through KT's. "I mean, Bijou uses more war paint, but underneath you have the same look."

"Most people don't see it."

Gwen shrugged. "I have an eye for detail. Do you know Lola Carmichael?"

"Should I?"

The woman chuckled. "She's a famous romance author, but fortunately she doesn't have much of an ego. She volunteers here, too."

Gwen led her to one side where a beautiful blonde sat in deep conversation with a boy, both their heads bent over a notebook. They were so engrossed that they didn't notice them until Gwen touched the blonde's shoulder.

The romance writer looked up, brow furrowed. Then her gaze flicked to KT, and her frown cleared into a smile. "You're Bijou's sister. I've heard a lot about you."

"None of it is true." KT pursed her lips and considered. "Except the story about me pushing Rod Stewart into the swimming pool."

They both laughed. Gwen turned to Lola. "KT is here to teach piano."

The laughter faded from Lola's face. "To Ashley?"

"Yeah."

The writer looked at her with pity. "Good luck with that."

She looked between the two women. "What haven't I been told here?"

"Ashley is just spirited," Gwen said. "She has a good heart."

"Uh-oh," KT said under her breath.

Lola smiled ruefully at her. "That's what I'm talking about."

Gwen showed her to a room at the back where there was a battered upright and a Goth girl leaning on the keys, looking bored.

KT stifled a groan. "Is that Ashley?"

"She's actually a sweet girl." Gwen wrinkled her nose. "Underneath all the black eyeliner and the dog collar."

She nodded, not convinced. It wasn't the nose ring or dog collar, which was kind of cool actually, or the all-black wardrobe. It was the look on her face, all teenage disdain, and the way she started sullenly jabbing A-minor over and over the moment she saw them approaching.

Next to her, Gwen sighed. Then her smile brightened determinedly and she said, "Ashley, this is your piano teacher, KT."

The girl looked up, her scowl fierce.

KT pulled a stool alongside the piano. No way was she sitting on the bench with the little viper. Gesturing to Gwen that she had this, she waited until the woman was gone before leaning toward the girl and lowering her voice. "First of all, cut out the act. I know that tactic. I use it all the time. You're not going to scare me away."

The girl looked at her disdainfully and hit the key harder. "Whatev."

She put her hand over the girl's to stop the noise. "I can tell you don't really want to be here so let's just get something straight, Ashley."

The girl lifted her elfin chin. "Call me Spike."

KT rolled her eyes. "Fine, Spike. I don't care whatever you did to land you here. I need to pretend to teach you music, and you need to pretend to learn, so suck it up and let's get on with this."

Ashley glared at her. "You're not touchy-feely like the other adults here."

"No, I'm not." She sat back and crossed her arms. "So you want to learn how to play or not?"

"Not." The girl mimicked her pose, sitting back and glaring.

"Fine." KT just stared at her steadily.

She thought that Ashley would lower her gaze after a while, but she was impressed that the girl kept up the staring match. It went on the whole time they were supposed to be learning scales. At the end of the hour she watched Ashley huff off.

"Interesting teaching method," Gwen said from the doorway with a smile on her face.

"Stay tuned for next time when I show her how to not read notes."

"It's hard sometimes at first, but she'll come around. She wants this."

That she found hard to believe. "If you say so."

Gwen laughed. "See you here on Friday."

"Unfortunately."

Still chuckling, the woman wandered away.

KT liked Gwen. She shouldn't have been surprised — Bijou was a good judge of character, except for that jerk she'd dated, Brice Bryland. But he'd been a blip on the screen. KT supposed everyone, even Bijou, showed a lapse of judgment sometime.

On her way home, she checked her messages. One from Bijou trying to get her to go to a therapist and three from her mother about trying on dresses for the concert.

Like hell.

Afraid that they'd be lying in wait for her at her cottage, she had the cab driver drop her off at the Carrington-Wright's. She let herself in through the kitchen, smiling when she saw that Celeste, their cook, had left out a plate of cookies for her. Chocolate chip, of course.

She grabbed two cookies and headed to the spare bedroom where she normally hid. It had a big, comfy bed in the sun for naps and the largest TV known to mankind with a million cable stations. Her parents didn't believe in TV, so they didn't have any. KT always thought about getting one, but she never got around to shopping for it.

The door to her room was closed. Strange. She shrugged and opened it, plopping on the bed straight away as she munched on a cookie. She reached for the remote on the bedside table.

Her fingers landed on a watch. A man's watch.

Frowning, she sat up and looked around the room. The room wasn't as tidy as usual. Men's clothing piled on a chair and one Nike running shoe forgotten in the middle of the room.

Someone was staying in her room? The only person staying with Elise, as far as she knew, was Chance.

Belatedly, KT registered the sound of running water in the attached bathroom—and the sound of stillness with it stopped. Was Chance in there?

It took nothing for her mind to picture him naked with water running down his body. In her mind, she saw him from behind, his broad shoulders narrowing to a vee at his waist. His butt was muscled and taut.

Wait—she gave him a tattoo of a spade on his left ass cheek. Perfect.

The bathroom door rattled, startling her out of her daydream.

Eyes wide, she started to scoot off the bed.

But then the door swung open, and Chance and his pig emerged.

Everyone froze.

Her eyes fell to the towel, hanging low on his hips. He was lean and muscled, with sexy abs like David Beckham's. She had first-hand experience with Beckham's abs — because of her parents, of course. They hung out poolside with him and Victoria every summer.

Chance's body was way sexier than Beckham's. She should have imagined him from the front.

What was she thinking? She should stop staring.

Yeah, right. KT had to swallow a few times before she could speak. "This is my room."

He raised his brows. "I thought you lived next door."

"Yeah, but this is my hideout." She frowned. "There are a million rooms in this house. Elise put you in this one?"

"I liked the bed." He studied her, his hand holding the towel in place. "I like it better now, though."

She flushed, her cheeks burning, as she read

his thoughts. They weren't far off from hers.

Except they weren't really dating. But if they were . . .

She needed not to think about things like that. She rushed off the bed so quickly she tumbled off.

He didn't seem to notice. He opened a drawer and pulled out underwear, the tight boxer kind in gray.

She liked gray.

"I, um"—she tripped over her feet—"have to go."

He turned around. His towel slipped a little. "Are you sure?"

"Yes." Because things didn't seem very pretend at the moment, and they'd definitely stop being pretend if she stayed. "See you around."

The pig, Ante Up, snorted as she left. To her ears, it sounded like he was laughing at her. Frankly, she couldn't blame him.

Chapter Eight

"YOU HAD A visitor yesterday."

Chance looked up from reading news on his phone, still surprised after the two weeks he'd been there to have someone talk to him. He and Elise had formed a late morning ritual of sorts. Since she woke up much earlier than him, she joined him for tea as he had his breakfast.

It didn't surprise him, though, that she'd know about KT's visit. Elise Carrington-Wright was a matriarch, and she had a finger in everything around her.

But that didn't mean he was going to make it easy for her. "What sort of visitor?"

"A female visitor."

He recognized that Elise was testing him in some way. It wouldn't surprise him if she were disapproving of him using KT as a decoy girlfriend. It sounded as though KT grew up in this house as much as her own.

Except KT felt like more than a decoy—he was going to remain hopeful about how much more. Until then, he was going to tread cautiously. "Oh?"

Elise eyed him over the rim of her teacup. "Don't play dumb with me, Chance. I've reared a son."

Chance grinned. "I thought I was playing clueless rather than dumb."

"It all amounts to the same result." She gave him a flat look. "Do you want to know who she was?"

He pictured KT's cat eyes and open face, felt the residual heat of her kisses, and his chest filled with electric warmth. "I think I know."

Frowning, Elise set down her cup. "I hope you're not taking up with her."

"Why do you say that?" he asked carefully, wondering if she was disapproving of KT or him.

"A mother's intuition. She seems desperate."

A lot of adjectives came to mind but desperate wasn't one of them. "KT?"

"No, that headhunter who's been sniffing around you." A spark of interest lit her expression. "What's this about KT?"

"Nothing." He leaned over and gave his attention to Ante Up, who lay lazily on the floor next to his untouched food bowl, like he'd had a night of debauchery. "Eat your vegetables."

The pig lifted his head and gave him a pitying look before lowering it and closing his eyes.

"That's not going to work, Chance. I'm not easily distractible." Elise put a hand on his arms, leaning toward him with an unholy gleam in her eyes. "Tell me why you'd assume Karma came over to see you."

He couldn't very well tell Elise of all people that he and KT were pretending to date. She lived next door to the Taylors—she had to be on somewhat friendly terms with them. He couldn't chance KT's parents finding out about their deal. But he felt bad about deceiving Elise, who in the past two weeks had become like his mother.

Would it really be deceiving her though? Because if he and KT were going out in any way, it was technically dating. And, quite frankly, there was nothing pretend about their kisses.

Elise put her hand on his. "I adore KT. She and Prescott have been friends forever, and she's a lovely, loyal girl. I don't know why I didn't see it before. Did you meet at the wedding?"

"After," he said, smiling at the memory of her toppling over the dividing hedge between the houses.

"She's amazingly talented. It's too bad she's built such a shell around herself."

"What sort of shell?"

"That's something you should ask her." Elise raised a brow. "In any case, it wasn't KT who came looking for you."

Chance winced. "Tiffany Woods is vetting me for the job I want."

"That's not all she's vetting you for." Elise didn't even bother to try to hide her amused smile. "Really, darling, no wonder you and Prescott are friends. It's like his high school days all over again, with girls coming to visit him."

"I didn't ask Tiffany to come."

She raised her brow. "Did you ask her not to?"

No, because he couldn't bring himself to reject someone who felt lonely, not when he knew what it felt like. "I told her I'm seeing KT."

"Are you really seeing KT? Because a woman

will be able to smell a ruse."

Remembering their first kiss, he nodded. "I think I was fairly convincing."

"Really?" Elise watched him with interest. "You'll have to tell me about that one day."

Chance flushed, not sure he could tell Elise that.

"Now I'm definitely curious." Chuckling, she rose from the table. "I suggest you nip this Tiffany Woods in the bud. She's the sort of woman who could cause problems down the road."

"Yeah, I can see that."

She raised her brows. "Do you? I've known women like her, Chance. A woman who's so aggressive she stalks a man doesn't understand normal boundaries. This one seems especially ruthless, if she's stalking you at home."

His phone rang and when he looked at the screen he winced. "Speak of the devil."

"I'll let you deal with her." Elise patted his shoulder, giving him a pitying look. "Good luck. You'll need it."

Taking a deep breath, he answered the call.

Before he could say anything, Tiffany said,

"Chance, Roger and I were just talking about you. Were your ears burning?"

Or something.

Tiffany continued, so he didn't have time to formulate a response. "Roger asked me to touch base with you. He's going out of town tonight for a couple days, but he'd like to see you when he returns."

"That sounds great." He wondered what the catch was.

"In the meantime, he asked me to keep you interested," she purred over the line.

There was the other shoe dropping. He smiled ruefully. "Roger doesn't have to worry."

"I like to be thorough, Chance," she said. "Let me take you to lunch to woo you."

"That's nice of you, but I'm looking at apartments today," he said honestly, relieved that he'd made the appointment with the rental broker.

"Would you like me to come along?" she offered, like a spider inviting a fly into her web. "I can reschedule lunch for another time. I know the city, and a woman's perspective can only be a good thing."

"My girlfriend is coming along," he said way more naturally than he'd have expected. "Thanks though."

"Next time." Her undercurrent of annoyance was mostly disguised.

Not if he could help it, he thought, but he put a smile in his voice. "Sure. Talk to you soon."

He hung up quickly and then, to make it legit, he called KT. "What are you doing?" he asked when she picked up the phone.

"Are you going to be the type of boyfriend who's always hovering?" she asked, her voice amused.

He grinned, feeling something inside him fall into place. "Are you saying you need your space?"

"You see, that's why I'm dating you, because you're so astute."

He chuckled. "Is that the only reason?"

"You kiss kind of nicely, too." Her voice lowered with desire.

His body reacted to it. "I didn't call to talk about kissing."

"Too bad."

He knew he had a goofy smile on his face, but

he didn't care. "But if you come with me to look at an apartment, I'll make sure you're rewarded with them."

"It's a deal."

"I'll pick you up at noon." He hung up, feeling good.

Ante Up snorted.

He reached down to scratch the little guy behind his ears. "You're just jealous. Maybe we can find you a fine companion of your own."

The pig jerked his snout in the air.

"Don't knock it. It's nice having a girlfriend." Even if she was a pretend one.

**It was before noon when he headed to KT's. Yeah, he was a little eager.

He wound his way through the side garden to the back of the house, following the directions she'd texted him. Apparently she lived in a separate unit from the rest of her family. It made sense. KT was an independent woman.

Her cottage was charming, if small, but it was the music that poured out from it that caught his attention. At first he thought it was a recording she was playing loudly, but as he got closer, he heard a pause and then the music resumed.

It was KT playing, he realized. He approached quietly and tested the door. Unlocked. He let himself in silently, not wanting to disturb her—not wanting her to stop.

The piano dominated the space, standing in the middle of the room. There were other instruments around the room; a violin seemingly at the ready. To the left there was a small kitchen that overlooked the room, and then a small hall that had a couple other doors and what looked like a messy bedroom at the end.

She sat at a larger-than-life grand piano, sheet music scattered on top of the piano in front of her. Her eyes were closed, and she rocked with the force of the song she played. The music rose in a powerful tide of emotion from the belly of the instrument, profound and layered. Powerful.

He let KT's passion wrap around him, feeling an echoing thrum in his chest as he watched her play. She was totally immersed, a single-minded focus that had him jealous of the piano.

In that moment, he knew he was going to make love to her. Of course he'd thought of it before—often—of stripping her bare and coaxing beautiful sounds from her, the same way she did with the piano. A man didn't buy lingerie for a woman if he didn't hope to see her in it.

Now he knew it was inevitable, no matter how temporary they claimed their relationship to be.

The music stopped with a crash, pulling him out of his carnal thoughts.

KT whirled around, fury in her eyes. "What are you doing here?"

"I came to pick you up." She looked like a caged animal and instinct told him not to bring up her music right now. He made his face blank, looked at his watch, and said, "We should go. I don't want to be late to meet the agent."

KT obviously struggled with what to say but then she stood up. "I know you were listening," she muttered as she grabbed her jacket.

"Why does that make you angry?"

"I told you I hate playing for people."

"You were playing for yourself, and I'm not

people. What happened that made you hate an audience so much?"

"Nothing." She pushed by him.

He took her arm and stopped her. "If I tell you it was the most beautiful music I've ever heard, would you still be angry at me for eavesdropping?"

"I don't know. Do you mean it?"

"Unequivocally."

She studied him as if trying to gauge his sincerity.

"I wouldn't lie to you, Karma."

She scowled but didn't move to retract her arm from his grip. "Call me Karma again and I'll punch you."

"I just wanted to get your attention." He smiled. "For someone who plays such passionate music, you're kind of gruff."

She flipped him off.

Laughing, he led her outside. While she locked the door, he asked, "What was that music?"

She flashed him a suspicious sidelong glance. "Why?"

"Because I have a feeling you won't play it for

me again and I really want to listen to it. It was amazing. I'll look for a recording of it."

She mumbled something.

"What?" he asked, leaning closer to hear her.

She mumbled again, but louder this time. "I wrote it."

Chance stopped in his tracks. "You?"

"Why do you look like it's so inconceivable?" she asked with grouchy irritation. "My parents are Anson and Lara. Music is in my DNA."

He pointed back at her cottage. "That wasn't music. That was . . . wow."

A range of emotions flickered across her face: pleasure, fear, hope, and stubborn resignation.

He wondered where the fear came from, and what happened to make someone who played like that refuse to let anyone listen. He wanted to ask her, but he could read people, and he knew without a doubt she'd just push him away.

One day she'd bare herself to him—physically and emotionally. He didn't know why, but that was important to him.

He kept their conversation light and innocuous as he drove them to the appointment in his borrowed car. The apartment wasn't far, in an area called Cow Hollow, just northeast of Laurel Heights.

The rental agent was already there showing the apartment to another couple when they arrived. Chance took KT's hand as he introduced her to the woman, mostly because he wanted to be closer to her. To the agent, he said, "I wanted to get KT's approval, because you never know when she might move in. Right, sweet pea?"

KT shot him a look. "It seems premature, doesn't it, honey bunny? Since we only met two days ago."

He squeezed her hand. "When it's right, it's right."

The real estate woman didn't seem to know what to do with them, so she pointed out the obvious things about the apartment, like the spare bedroom and extra closet space. When they reached the top floor, she showed them how all the windows in the living room tinted to protect against the sun.

KT rolled her eyes at him but then she faked enthusiasm, saying, "It's not going to be a living room for long. It's perfect for my piano," she purred.

"Karma has a grand piano," he explained to the wide-eyed real estate agent.

"Hey," his "girlfriend" protested. "It's not just a grand piano, it's a Pleyel. It deserves respect." She turned to the agent. "How do the windows work? Direct sun is the kiss of death for instruments."

"Here." The agent pressed a button on the wall and all the windows darkened automatically.

KT patted his belly. "That must please your masculine heart. Men like gadgets like that."

"It is instant privacy." He pulled her closer. "We won't have to worry about the neighbors watching."

The agent cleared her throat. "I'll just let you look around," she said, quickly leaving the room.

KT gave him a look and pushed away from him to explore. "This is amazing," she said, walking into the bathroom. "Look at the tub. Half the Giants could take a bath at once."

"Like it here then?"

She glanced at him, wary. "You don't have to

keep pretending when it's just us."

"I'm not pretending." Locking the door, he went up behind her and slid his arms around her waist. He nibbled her neck and felt her go liquid in his arms. Because he couldn't help it, he trailed his hand lower, testing, and when she didn't protest or hit him, he undid her jean button and slid his hand in.

Chapter Nine

KT HELD HER breath as his fingers slid down further into her pants. They slipped under her panties, ruffling her hair.

Her back arched of its own accord. "This seems to be crossing the line into reality."

"Do you have a problem with that?" he asked softly.

She probably should, but she really didn't. "You know I don't."

He dipped one finger into her.

She gasped as he touched the right spot and starbursts broke out behind her lids. She linked her arms behind his head and rubbed her hips against the prominent bulge in his pants. "You're happy to see me."

"Of course I am. You're all I think about lately." He focused his touch, rubbing softly but insistently. His other hand snaked under her top. His palm paused over her breast before he covered it with his entire warm hand. "You aren't wearing a bra again."

"It seems pointless when I barely have anything going on."

"You have plenty going on." He rolled her nipple gently between his fingers, squeezing just enough to cause her to gasp. "Have you been braless every time we've been together?"

"Yes."

"Are you trying to kill me? You know that's dangerous knowledge to have, right?" He pushed her shirt up, baring her.

They both looked in the mirror. The tips of her breasts were dark red, pointy and hard. He trailed his tanned hand up, running his long fingers over them, one by one. They both watched as he focused on one and teased it harder.

Her eyes dipped lower, seeing his other hand hidden by her pants but feeling everything he was doing. "This is really . . ."

His lips trailed up her neck to just below her ear. "What is it? Tell me."

"Exciting." Admitting it made her feel on the edge. Suddenly, her climax felt around a very short corner. She gripped his hair, arching back against him. "You're going to make me come," she whispered, meeting his gaze.

"Over and over," he promised, biting her neck as he focused his finger on just the right spot.

She tensed, losing control as her body took over. She squeezed her eyes shut as the orgasm hit her. She writhed against him, wanting more, wishing he were filling her at the same time.

As her heart began to slow down, she heard people outside the door. Her eyes flew open, meeting Chance's in the mirror as she remembered where they were and that there were other people in the apartment. She swallowed. "Have they been there the whole time?"

"I'm not sure. I was busy," he said.

She shivered as his finger slid slowly over her as he withdrew his hand. He turned her around and lowered his head to lick her nipple. He was enthusiastic and unapologetic about it, hungry for her.

She gasped, feeling needy all over again, like she hadn't just had her mind blown. "I think I need more."

"How about we go to a place where there are fewer people walking through? Like my boat."

"Your boat?" She perked up. "Okay."

He gave the tip of her breast one last love bite and then pulled her shirt down. After redoing her jeans, he washed his hands and adjusted himself before unlocking the door and letting them out.

Just beyond the bathroom, the agent and another couple watched them with wide eyes.

His hand on KT's back, Chance pointed behind them as he propelled her forward. "It's great in there. You should try it."

KT tried not to snicker but failed. By the time they were out of the apartment and on the sidewalk, they were both laughing.

Chance caught her up and kissed her, their laughs mingling into one. "Let's go, sweet pea."

**KT wasn't a stranger to boats. She'd been on her fair share all around the world. But Chance's boat was charming and felt homey from the moment she stepped on board, despite its name.

"Blow Job?" KT asked with a raised brow as she toed off her shoes.

Standing behind her, his hands slipped under her clothing, up to cup her breasts. "I'm going to assume you're talking about the boat as opposed to offering. It's a sailboat. Wind, blow . . . Get it?"

She reached behind, pulling him closer to her. "Punny."

"It's the name the boat came with. I keep meaning to change it."

"Maybe we can take this conversation and everything else inside." It was a nice afternoon and lots of tourists walked down the Marina. "People are watching."

"I'd unlock the cabin and let us in, but you keep distracting me." He undid her pants. Again.

She arched back. "I think you're the one doing the distracting."

"Nope. I'm right on this one." He unwound from her, unlocked the padlock, and opened the cabin below. Taking her hand, he guided her down the narrow stairs. "We're inside. Get naked."

"You're not the boss of me," she said as she shrugged her jacket off and dropped it on the floor.

"No, I'm not, but I wouldn't be surprised to

find out that you're my boss." He pulled his shirt over his head.

"Geez, you're nice to look at." She tossed her shirt aside and began to push her pants and underwear off. "You work out?"

"You want to talk about my exercise regime now?"

"Would it be more appropriate to ask if you happen to have a tattoo of a spade on your ass cheek?"

"How about if I show you?" he said as he got rid of the rest of his clothes.

She almost tripped over her shoes as she surveyed his naked form. He really was perfect — ripples of muscles and an impressive erection that jutted toward her, as if it yearned for her too. "No tattoo."

"Are you disappointed?"

There was nothing to be disappointed about here. She ran her tongue along her lip. "So, couch? Bed? Against the wall?"

"Have I told you I love how your mind works?" He sat on the steps they'd just descended and held his arms out. In his hand was a condom. "Take me."

She looked at the condom, not entirely sure how to tackle it. The guy always did it. But with Chance spread out like a feast, all for her, she wasn't going to let a little bit of rubber stop her from enjoying.

As if he sensed her hesitation, he said, "Come sit on me."

She did—eagerly. His thighs felt strong under her, and she ran her hands along his muscled chest.

He ripped open the package with his teeth and held it out. "Pinch the tip and roll it over me."

"I can do that," she said, taking it.

He smiled. "Yes, you can."

She did just that, slowly, liking the way his eyes glazed over and his hips jutted up eager for her touch.

He dropped his head back. "You're killing me."

"Don't die yet." She unrolled the condom all the way down and then surveyed her handiwork. "We're just getting to the fun stuff."

"You're right." He gripped her hips. "Climb on me."

She did, not caring that she was graceless. She just wanted him in.

He exhaled as she worked herself down on him. "One day, Karma, I'm going to take you against the wall, and in a bed. And even on your piano."

"My piano is sacred," she said, her hands running over him.

"Exactly." He brought her closer to kiss her, dark drugging kisses that made her head spin.

The boat rocked. She wasn't sure if it was from the motion of the bay or the rhythm of their love. She dropped her head back, inhaling the salt air and she looked up and saw blue sky. Gripping him, feeling joy, she laughed.

"What is it?" he asked against her neck.

"I'm delirious." She swivelled her hips against him, gasping at the hot rush of feeling sparking between them.

"You're going to come again," he said, tugging her head back by her hair. "I feel it."

"Yes." She closed her eyes, hands propped on his chest. She felt his hands, the lick of his tongue, a stray finger — all encouraging her.

"Come with me, Karma," he whispered. "Come with me."

She didn't have a choice. She came so strongly she couldn't make a sound, feeling him tighten and rush to join her. At the end, she lay on top of him, trying to catch her breath.

He traced a hand down her spine, to her hip, shifting her into him.

She frowned though she couldn't lift her head. "Are you still hard?"

"It wasn't enough." He ever-so-slowly pushed himself into her over and over.

She sighed. "This is —"

"Lightning in a bottle," he finished for her.

She couldn't have put it better.

Chapter Ten

WILL OPENED HIS office door. "Hi Bijou."

Her heart flopped seeing his smile, like she was in a love song of her own. She stood up, rubbing her palms on her white jeans.

"Where's KT?" he asked, looking around his waiting room as if her sister could be hiding somewhere.

"I need to talk to you about that." She walked inside, trying not to shiver as she brushed by him.

His cell phone rang. He looked at the screen and winced. "I need to take this. Grab a seat and relax, I'll be right back."

Nodding as he walked out, she dropped her bag by the couch. She wandered to the bookshelf. She expected to see psychology books and self-help titles like What Color is Your Parachute? There were a few books like that but there were also travel books and—

"Sheet music?" Frowning, she pulled out a book of Cole Porter standards. A strange choice for a therapist. She flipped through it stopping at "Night and Day." Great song.

Smiling, she put the book back, humming it to herself. Her gaze fell to the shelf below where there were a few framed pictures. She stooped down to study them. In the first one, Will stood with Wynton Marsalis's arm around him like they were great buddies. In another, he and Bruce Springsteen held up their glasses in a toast to each other. The picture frame at the end showed Will on stage playing a guitar with Eric Clapton.

He was a musician.

"Sorry about that," Will said as he re-entered his office. "You were going to tell me where KT is."

Bijou picked up the picture and held it out. "You're a musician."

"I play, yes." He closed the door, his brow furrowing. "Does that bother you?"

"Hell, yes, it bothers me." She set the photo back down and began to pace. "Musicians suck."

"That's a little ironic, considering you're one, isn't it?" he asked with a dry smile.

"Don't make this about me." She glared at him. "You lied to me."

"Wait a minute." He sobered, stepping forward with his hand outstretched. "I missed something here. How do you think I've lied to you?"

"I don't just think it." She pointed at the picture. "You played on stage with Clapton?"

"A couple times, yes. Does that bother you?"

"Stop trying to shrink me." She stopped in front of him, hands on her hips. "I'm so disappointed in you. I actually liked you."

"And now, because I can play a guitar, you don't?" he asked cautiously.

She jabbed a finger at his chest. "Don't you dare imply that I'm irrational."

"Of course not."

"And don't placate me." She poked him with her fingertip again, glaring. "I actually liked you."

"You said that." He took her hand and cupped it in his. "Want to sit down and tell me what's underneath all this anger?"

"No, I don't." She pulled her hand free, not because he was trying to analyze her but because it was making her brain scramble. She couldn't think or hold on to her anger while he touched her.

Which made her angrier. Why did she have such a weakness when it came to men like him? She began to pace, trying to focus on the goal here, which wasn't getting in his pants even if that was what she thought about each time she saw him.

"Bijou."

She glared at him. "Don't say my name like that."

He shook his head; his brow furrowed with confusion. "Like what?"

Like he wanted to lick her head to toe. She threw her hands in the air. "I don't know why I'm surprised you're a musician. I mean, look at you. You're totally hot."

"And this bothers you."

"Of course it bothers me. I liked you."

"So you've said." His expression was somber, but she saw the humor in his eyes.

She narrowed her eyes. "Don't mock me. I'm really annoyed at the moment."

"I had a clue or two." He smiled overtly this time. Then he took her arm. "Why does me being a musician bother you so much, Bijou?"

"Because I'm only ever attracted to musicians," she admitted helplessly. She touched his skin where it was exposed at his collar. "I mean, look at you. I thought you were hot and edgy when you were just a therapist. Now I'm completely screwed."

"Bijou," he said in his calm voice. "Let's just talk this out. It's not —"

"There's nothing to talk out." She stepped out of his magnetic field so she could think. "Do you make house calls?"

He looked at her silently, speculation in his gaze.

"Not for me, for KT." She glared at him. "And don't look at me like that. Therapists aren't supposed to look at people that way."

"What way is that?"

"Like you're picturing me answering the door in a tiny scrap of lace when you make your house call."

He quirked his brow and folded his arms. "Maybe you're the one picturing it."

Oh, yes, she was. She was wearing the barely-there negligee she bought in Paris last year, and he was on his knees in front of her, in awe.

She flushed. "Stop distracting me. This is about KT."

"I don't typically make house calls," he said in his damn soothing voice, taking a seat. "Maybe you should sit down, and we can talk about what has you so upset."

"What has me upset is that I can't seem to break out of a destructive pattern." She glared at him. "I blame you."

He raised his brows. "Why?"

"Because you look like—" She waved her hand at him.

"A musician?"

"Yes. It's like you're a human chocolate bar, and I want to eat every last bit."

"And that's bad?"

"I won't eat musicians." Pouting, she dropped onto the couch and lay down on her back, arm across her eyes. "Let's just focus on KT."

"Why are you so intent on bringing KT to see me when she clearly isn't interested?"

She pounded her fist on the couch. "Because my future is at stake here. If KT doesn't get her act together, Mom won't let me perform at their concert either, and I have everything riding on this."

"Why do you need to prove yourself so badly?"

"This isn't about proving myself."

"It's not?"

She scowled at him. "I'm really starting to hate when you answer me with questions."

He smiled. "I've heard that once or twice."

"I don't think it's wrong for me to want to re-alize my destiny."

"Of course not, but at what price?" He shifted. "It's also good to know why you want it so badly."

"Why didn't you want to be a working musi-cian? You're obviously really good if you're play-ing with Clapton and Springsteen."

"We were talking about you."

"You were, but you're more interesting.." She turned on her side and propped her head up with her hand. "What makes someone who's that good go into therapy instead?"

"Bijou, we're not here to talk about me."

"Well, we're not here to talk about me either, despite what you think."

He studied her. She couldn't read his thoughts

and that bothered her. It felt like she should know what he was thinking.

"I'll make you a deal," he said finally. "You tell me why it's so important for you to prove yourself and I'll tell you why I went into therapy."

"I want to prove I'm better than Brice Bryland," she heard herself say. She covered her mouth, shocked that she said it, and looked at him.

Will's brow furrowed. "Brice Bryland is a musical hack. Why would you care if you're better than him?"

"He stole my song." She swallowed thickly and sat down on the edge of the couch, leaning her elbows on her knees and staring at her hands. "We dated for longer than we should have and during that time I wrote a song about us. He convinced me to record it as a duet but then he recorded it on his own behind my back. But that's not the worst part."

"What is?"

She looked at Will, hearing a hint of something in his voice she couldn't identify. If she didn't know better, she'd have sworn it was jealousy. "Brice stole my magic. I haven't been able to write since. The label fired me for breach of contract, and I've spent the past year trying to get it back."

"Your parents —"

She shook her head. "I don't want to ride on their coattails, but it's expected to a certain degree. I mean, I can't get away from the fact that I'm Anson and Lara's daughter, but I want to rise to the top because of my own skills. The label is going to be at this concert, and it's my chance to show them what they've lost. They'll take me back if they see I'm back on top."

He nodded thoughtfully. "But do you really want a label that didn't have your back to sign you up again? What makes you think they won't dump you at the next sign of adversity?"

"Ouch." She winced. "Don't pull your punches, Doc. Tell it to me like it is."

"It's how I roll." He grinned, and her heart stopped. As she tried to breathe again, he asked, "What's your plan if your former label doesn't come through?"

"That's not an option," she replied firmly. Not even the fact that she hadn't been able to write for a year was going to stop her.

"So you're going to bulldoze your way into success."

"You say that like it's a bad thing."

He shrugged. "It's certainly a lot of work."

"My path is mostly carved out. I just have to clear the brush."

"Paths change." He stretched his legs out, straightened his pant legs. "I used to be a musician, you know, but I helped a friend of mine who had issues with stage fright get over it, and I realized I liked that. So I went to school and got my degree. I still love music, but this is my calling. I make a difference in the world in a way I never did playing guitar, though I still get to do that, too."

"You picked a different path," she concluded.

"Exactly."

An alarm chimed softly.

"Our time's up," he said, standing up.

"You sound reluctant instead of relieved." She picked up her purse and followed him to the door.

"I enjoy talking to you." He took her hand. "I actually like you, too."

She looked in his eyes and something zapped her right in the middle of her chest.

"To be clear," he said softly, "you don't want to be my patient."

"No, I don't," she replied, her voice breathy.

"Good." His gaze lowered to her lips, and he leaned toward her.

He was going to kiss her.

Her lips parted, and her heart hammered.

But she jerked herself back. Bad idea. He was a therapist now, but he was a musician at heart. She couldn't chance being distracted that way again. The last time had set her back catastrophically.

She stepped backward, bumping into the door. "I should go. I need to, um, do something."

He smiled, opening the door for her, still holding her hand. As she slipped past him, he held her back. "Bijou, your magic was never gone. You're trying hard for something you already have."

"My label doesn't think so."

"Record execs are idiots. Anyone looking at you can tell you're made of magic."

She swallowed thickly, at a loss for words at the complete faith she saw in his expression.

Oh hell. She grabbed his shirt and kissed him,

a quick brush against his lips that left her wanting more. Much, much more.

She turned and strode out before she could give in. She didn't need to get distracted, especially by an ex-musician who was her sister's would-be therapist, no matter how attractive and sweet he was.

Chapter Eleven

KT DRUMMED HER fingers on the decrepit piano. "Are you going to play or what, Spike?"

Ashley just studied her chipped black nail polish.

"Being a teenager is sucky," KT said. "I'm pretty sure I was a bitch back then, too."

The look the kid gave her clearly said, "Just back then?"

"You're right. I was a great teenager actually." She nodded to the piano. "I practiced my scales."

"Yeah, right," Ashley muttered, flicking a piece of nail polish onto the keys.

"Hey." KT leaned in, angry now, and got in the teenager's face. "You never disrespect your instrument. This piano is an extension of you. Treating it badly is like treating yourself badly. I don't care if you never give me, or anyone else, any respect, but you never treat the piano that way."

Ashley blinked in shock. "Fine. Geez. Back off."

Glaring, KT pointed at the keys. "Play."

She must have scared the kid a little because Ashley began to peck out a surly rendition of C-major. Better than nothing, she supposed, wincing at a particularly violent note.

"I don't know why we're doing this," Ashley muttered.

"I don't either. What am I doing here?"

The teenager glanced at her. "You mean besides making my life hell?"

"Yeah, because I'm pretty sure you can find lots of volunteers to torment you." KT crossed her arms. "Gwen said you wanted to learn the piano. Either you do or you don't. Which is it?"

"I do," was the eventual sullen reply. "Real things, not baby stuff like scales."

"You have to be able to walk before you can dance. Scales are walking. You're the one who wanted to learn to play the piano."

The kid gave her a sidelong glare. "I wanted a real teacher."

"Yeah, well, you got me, Spike." She grinned evilly.

Ashley made a face and banged on the keys,

albeit more gently than she had been. "I don't know why I'm bothering with this. You're just going to leave."

She felt a pang of guilt at that truth. "Who said I was going to leave?"

"Everyone leaves." Ashley shrugged as she started playing the scale over again. "Adults never keep their promises."

Who'd run out on this kid? KT studied the girl's profile, for the first time seeing the fragile hurt hidden behind the attitude and makeup.

She really didn't want to identify with the kid, but she couldn't help herself. The teenager was just as conscious of being judged as KT was, only instead of retreating the way KT did, Ashley hit everyone over the head with her uniqueness.

"You know what I promise you?" KT said finally.

"What?"

"To whoop your ass if you don't play C-major properly." She shook her head. "But, hey, it's amazing how you're able convey teen angst in every note. I don't know whether to be annoyed or impressed."

The girl rolled her eyes, but her lips pulled tight like she was trying not to smile.

KT threw her arms in the air. "The apocalypse is nigh!"

"What?" Ashley looked at her like she was insane.

"The apocalypse must be approaching, because you're almost smiling."

The kid rolled her eyes again, but this time as she began her scales, they were softer and more melodic with breathing and emotion that wasn't bordering on fury.

It was good—really good.

KT sat up and paid attention. Ashley's hand positioning sucked, but some great pianists had wonky positioning. It was the tone that mattered, and Ashley was coaxing the sorry-excuse-for-a-piano to sing like an angel.

"That's not bad," KT said, underplaying how impressed she felt.

"Like I care what you think," Ashley mumbled, her head lowered.

Only the girl had to care. No one played boring scales like that if they were indifferent. KT had hated practicing her scales when she was a kid.

The teenager looked up at her with a scowl. "What are you staring at?"

She had the urge to hug the kid, which would have weirded them both out, so instead she said, "I'm staring at a brat who can't play C-major. Want to try A-minor? It's totally mournful, like you."

The girl's eyes narrowed. "You're wretched."

"And you're stuck with me, so deal." She crossed her arms and waited.

Ashley heaved a sigh. "Fine. Show me A-minor."

Hiding a triumphant smile, KT launched into a convoluted explanation of minor chord progressions that was sure to drive the teenager insane. It was the little pleasures that made life sweet.

**KT shook her head as she left the Purple Elephant. She'd never have expected it, but they'd actually had a good session. Surprisingly, Ashley tolerated the lecture.

Not just tolerated—the girl may have pretended to be disinterested but KT could tell she was paying attention. She'd gotten so into the discussion that she forgot about irritating the teenager and launched into a discussion about theory. Ashley had soaked it all up like a sponge.

It'd been weird.

She flagged down a taxi, feeling jazzed. On impulse, she called Chance. "What are you wearing?" she asked the moment he answered the phone.

"A towel and a smile," he replied.

Remembering how he looked in a towel, she squirmed in the torn backseat of the cab. "I'll be right over in that case."

"Good." He hung up.

She slipped the phone in her pocket and leaned into the divider between her and the driver. "Step on it."

He glanced at her in the rearview mirror and rolled his eyes, not going any faster.

Well, she tried.

San Francisco wasn't super big, so she arrived at the Carrington-Wright house quickly anyway. She paid the driver and hopped out.

Chance and Ante Up were waiting for her

on the front stoop. His hair was damp, and he looked freshly shaven. Bummer that she missed the shower.

Lighting up when he saw her, he stood. "Hey."

"Hey." Playing it cool, she scratched the pig under his chin when really she wanted to launch herself at Chance.

He took her other hand and drew her into his chest. "I don't know how I should feel about you giving the little porker affection before me."

"Do you need affection?" She wound her arms around his neck.

"Always." Lowering his mouth, he kissed her.

It was just what she needed, too. She sighed, relaxing against him.

He gave her an Eskimo kiss. "I need to take Ante Up for a walk. Want to join us?"

"Walk?" She wrinkled her nose. "How far are you going, and are there hills?"

Chance groaned. "Not you, too."

Snorting, the pig waved his snout up and down.

"I know. He's talking crazy," KT said to Ante Up. Then she faced Chance and shrugged. "It seems like we outnumber you. I have a better solution."

They ended up at Li Po, a dive bar in Chinatown—without Ante Up, because they decided it was probably not a good idea to take a pig there. Ordering a couple beers, they sat at the bar.

"Ante Up is sorry to be missing this," Chance said, tapping his bottle to hers. "That pig loves his pale ales."

KT grinned. "He's a strange animal."

"Tell me about it."

"Since we're talking about strange animals, I had a session with the teenager I'm tutoring."

Chance angled his legs to bracket hers. "She's strange?"

"To say the least." KT pursed her lips in thought. "It's not her appearance as much as it's her attitude. She pretends to be snarky, but underneath I think she really wants to learn piano."

"If I had you as a teacher, I'd be eager to learn." He gave her an exaggerated leer as he lifted the beer bottle to his mouth.

"You'd sit there and think about what I was wearing under my clothes."

He leaned in and softly said, "I already know that you don't wear a bra."

She arched her brow at him and took a swig of her beer. "Maybe."

He stilled. "What does that mean?"

"Remember the bra and panties you bought me?"

"Do I ever." He swallowed audibly.

"Olivia was right. They aren't uncomfortable." She grinned at the way his eyes dropped, as if he was trying to see past the outer layer she wore. "Anyway," she said, "today was just a revelation. I feel like I got through to Ashley a little."

He shook his head. "I'm still stuck on your lingerie."

His phone rang, and he lifted it out to look at it. Then he silenced it and tucked it away.

"No one important?" she asked.

"No. Just Tiffany Woods. The headhunter," he explained at her blank look.

"She's determined."

He shrugged. "I don't understand why she's so bent on me."

"Is this job worth the aggravation?" KT leaned

her chin on her hand. "Aren't there other jobs you can apply for?"

"It's tough in this market, and I have no real work experience. Paragon is interested in people who have my unique abilities. In the Bay Area, cutting edge finance companies like that are few and far between." He faced her, putting his hand on her leg. "I know without a doubt that I want to be here."

She wanted him to be here. For someone who was just a pretend boyfriend, he meant a lot to her already. She put her hand on top of his, keeping him there. "Couldn't you keep playing poker instead of taking a job?"

"Not if I want to have a normal family life. And playing was never a forever thing. It was a temporary measure till I figured out what my purpose was."

"Your purpose?"

"The way I'm supposed to change the world." His expression sobered. "My dad used to tell me that everyone was meant to put their mark on the world, to change it for the better, and our life's journey was to figure out how."

She leaned in, interested. "So what's your purpose? To make money?"

"Pretty much." He smiled ruefully. "I take risky situations and find ways to win. Not the most politically correct purpose to have these days, but it's what I'm good at."

She wasn't surprised when Chance looked her in the eye and asked, "What's your purpose, KT?"

Music. The answer was immediate and irrefutable. But she just shrugged because she knew where this conversation would lead.

He squeezed her thigh. "Then what's your goal in life?"

"I don't have a goal." At his baffled look, she shrugged. "I don't need one. I'm happy as I am. It's worked for me so far."

"Aren't you working on anything?"

"Well, sure." She thought about her nearly-finished concerto.

"What are you going to do when you finish it?"

She frowned. "Is this a trick question? I'll start something else."

"And the project you're working on now?" At her blank look, he gestured with his hand. "Will

you perform it somewhere?"

"No." She shook her head vehemently. "I don't perform."

"Why not?"

She studied him, wondering how much she should say. She shocked herself by blurting, "I have stage fright."

His expression remained neutral, no judgement.

Which made it easier for her to continue. "When I was four, my parents were having one of their big parties. Mom wanted me to perform a song I'd written. She dressed me up in a fancy dress that itched and stuck me in the middle of the room."

Just thinking about it made her begin to feel sick again—she could hear the tinkle of glasses and the muffled laughter, and then, absurdly loud, one man's voice saying, Oh save me from another spoiled brat's god-awful recital.

People had laughed when she tripped and tore her dress, and then they'd laughed more when she couldn't climb on the piano bench because of the puffy layers of her dress. She couldn't play, paralyzed by the mocking laughter and the snide whispers.

"Hey." Chance lifted her chin. "You're not there anymore."

But she was—every time she was in front of people all those emotions reared up like a monster hiding under her bed, ready to eat her up. "And I'll never be again. It was humiliating."

"You were four," he pointed out gently. "Shouldn't you give yourself a break?"

She narrowed her eyes. "I don't perform. Period."

"So have someone else perform your music."

"I used to. They don't play it right."

"You must have a goal for the songs you compose." At her mutinous look, he gaped at her. "Seriously? You write them and then they don't see the light of day?"

"Now you sound like my mom."

"Maybe your mom is right."

She glared at him. "Careful, or I'll break up with you."

"You can't break up with me." He pulled her stool closer to his. "It's not a big deal if you don't want to play in front of people, but if your music is important to you, there are ways of getting it out."

"No label is going to sign an artist who won't perform."

"So stack the deck the way you want it. It's your hand, play it any way you want." He gestured to the disinterested bartender for another round. "Start your own label."

"Right." She smirked.

"I'm serious. Go indie. What do you have to lose?" He nodded in thanks and handed KT a fresh bottle. "Though if you don't feel compelled to have your music heard, maybe it's not your purpose."

Not her purpose? She blinked at the ridiculous thought.

But she knew she couldn't say anything to the contrary without backing herself into a corner.

She pouted.

He nudged her leg with his. "Maybe being a teacher is your calling."

"Ha! Unlikely." She considered it for two seconds and then shuddered in horror. "Not even."

"It was just a thought." He slid his hand up her

thigh. "I have another thought I guarantee you'll like better. It involves the fancy bra you're wearing and me taking it off."

"That's something I can get behind." She slid off the stool.

He caught her close, holding her gaze. "Maybe one day you'll play for me?"

"Maybe." Not.

His lips quirked, as if he could hear her thoughts. Placing a kiss on her forehead, he vowed, "One day you will, and I'll feel honored to be the one you trust."

The tight feeling in her chest constricted—not at the thought of playing for him, but that she'd hurt him by not playing.

Chapter Twelve

*B*IJOU STRODE TOWARD the carriage house with purpose, practicing what she was going to say to KT to convince her to go to therapy with her. Only as she approached the front door, what she heard made her lose her train of thought.

Music. But not just any music—the most haunting music she'd ever heard.

Her ear pressed to the door, she tried to place the melody, but she didn't recognize it. More complicated than Beethoven, less chirpy than Bach, more serious than Mozart. It was modern, but not Rachmaninov or Chopin, or even someone like Cage. There was a hint of the romanticism of Michael Nyman or Ennio Morricone, but without the sappy sentimentality. This was raw and powerful but still sweet.

She stood, cast in a spell by the rising music, when KT's voice rose from behind the piano, like the sun coming out from behind the clouds.

Her sister's voice was soft at first, mingling gently with the music, then suddenly soaring over the piano's voice, strong and commanding.

Bijou's heart thundered the same way it had when she'd kissed Will. Whatever this was, it was good. Why hadn't she heard it before?

Knowing KT hardly ever locked her door, Bijou quietly twisted the knob and let herself in.

Her sister sat at the piano, rocking as she sang. Her hair was the perfect kind of messy Bijou spent an hour to achieve. Her eyes were closed, and she belted out the words from her soul.

It'd have been so easy to be jealous of her sister. KT didn't realize it, but she was gorgeous and so talented it made Bijou's teeth ache. As close as they were in age, they'd never had any sort of rivalry, probably due to their parents, who'd always encouraged them to be themselves and had never compared them to each other. But she knew a lot had to do with KT and her unwavering loyalty and love.

The piano screeched to a halt. KT whirled around to glare at her. "What are you doing here?"

So much for the love, Bijou thought with a wry

grin. "I'm listening to you play. Before you explode in righteous indignation, tell me who the composer was."

"Why?"

"Because I've never heard it before, and it was amazing."

Her sister's eyes narrowed suspiciously. "Are you just saying that?"

She shook her head. "Why would I? When haven't I said if I thought something sucked?"

KT shrugged, looking indecisive. Then she muttered something.

"What?" Bijou cupped her ear and leaned forward.

"I wrote it, okay?" Her sister crossed her arms defiantly, glaring at her.

"You?" Bijou blinked. "Are you serious?"

KT's face stormed over. "Are you saying I don't have what it takes?"

"Of course not, but I've never heard you compose classical music before." Bijou took her sister's hand. "KT, that was the most amazing music I've ever heard."

"Are you just saying that to be nice?"

"When have I ever been nice?"

"Well, that's true."

She pushed KT's shoulder. Then she took her arms, shook her, and yelled, "That was the most amazing music ever! Karma Taylor, where did that come from?"

KT looked away, abashed but hopeful. "Really? You thought it was that good?"

"Don't you?"

Her sister suddenly grinned. "I think it's damn great."

Everything suddenly clicked. "This is why you haven't been worried about losing the gig with Jamila. You've been composing something different and all your own. Wait till Mom and Dad hear. They're going to flip."

"They aren't going to hear." KT grabbed her arms and looked her in the eyes. "You're not going to tell anyone about my concerto, Bijou. Swear it."

"You can't hide that." She pointed at the piano. "That won't be stifled."

"It's not ready yet." KT began to pace. "There's still a section I'm not happy with, and I haven't had much time to work on it. And you know Mom's just going to pressure me about it, and who can create under that sort of pressure. Really, it's—"

"KT." She put a hand on her sister's arm to stop her. "Breathe."

She exhaled raggedly. "I'm just not ready."

Bijou nodded, understanding that her sister felt that way, but at the same time wanting to call bullshit. KT was never ready. "Music that powerful can't be stifled. Isn't hiding something that beautiful a crime?"

Her sister shook her head. "It's just a concerto."

"It's not just anything." She held her sister's face in her hands. "I got goosebumps listening to it, and you know how jaded I am. That's the sort of music that changes lives."

KT shook free stubbornly. "You're being dramatic."

"I'm being serious. This can't be tucked away in a drawer, forgotten. You need to do something with it."

"That's the thing." KT frowned. "I haven't decided what."

"Do you have ideas?"

Her sister shot her a flat look. "It's not doing live performances, if that's where you're going with this. I'm considering other options."

Bijou wanted to ask what options, but she knew better than to push. "I hope you find the option that's right for you," she said, kissing KT's cheek, "because it's unforgettable."

⁂The concerto was so unforgettable, Bijou couldn't shake it from her mind. That music . . .

Goosebumps broke out down her arm as she remembered it. And then when KT's voice had joined it, adding another layer of haunting complexity.

Calling it a crime to hide it was an understatement. She walked down the driveway to her car, replaying it over and over in her mind.

It was general consensus in their family that KT was gifted, despite what KT herself thought. But they'd only based that on the pop music she wrote for other people and the rare moments they'd overheard her singing. None of them had any idea her true talent lay in neo-classical music.

Bijou stopped abruptly, staring unseeing at her car. KT's classical music could be her salvation.

It could save Bijou, too.

Not that KT would ever show her concerto to their mom, but Bijou could.

She bit her lip. KT might never forgive her if she did that. Of course, she might also be eternally grateful, because it'd get their mom off her back. If Lara knew KT had a classical focus, she'd let her off the hook for the concert. It was a rock concert, after all, not a night at the symphony.

"What are you doing, Ruby Red? Is something wrong with your car?"

She looked up to see her dad, hands in his pockets, glasses askew, watching her with bright interest. "I'm thinking, Daddy."

He tipped his head. "As long as you're plotting for the good of the world."

"It's for KT's good."

"Karma is a tricky creature." Anson pursed his lips. "She's always walked her own path, that girl."

"Mom doesn't think she's walking down that path fast enough."

A soft smile lit her dad's face. "Yes, well, Lara is her own creature, as well. Amazing woman. You're so much like her."

Bijou wished she could believe that. She

doubted her mom would ever have let someone steal her ability to create.

Her dad patted her arm. "Lara forgets some of us take longer to come into our own, but it'll all work out, sweetie. Your mom always makes sure of that."

She was going to make sure, too, because she had too much riding on this. "Do you ever wonder about your path and what would have happened if you hadn't met Mom?"

"If it weren't for her, I'd probably still be playing guitar on the corner of Haight and Ashbury. Karma and I are alike that way. We're happy to play our music for no one but ourselves. Lara thinks that talent shouldn't be bottled and put away, but I don't know." He shrugged, straightening his broken frames. "Who are we to say what's right or wrong for someone?"

Normally, Bijou would have agreed with him but not when her future was on the line—and especially not since telling their mom about KT's music would benefit them both.

That was a decision, she guessed.

Her dad tiptoed up to kiss her on the cheek.

"Your mother gets that look, too, and it's always my cue to run and hide. Do good, Ruby Red."

He didn't say it, but she heard the underlying words nonetheless: because karma was a bitch, and her Karma was going to be annoyed. But in the end she'd thank her. Bijou nodded confidently. She'd take care of both herself and her sister.

Chapter Thirteen

WHEN KT OPENED her door, her happy smile was for Chance. They were going out for dim sum and beer in Chinatown.

Only instead of Chance at her door, it was her mother. The bright look in her eyes made KT instantly wary. The fact that Bijou brought up the rear looking very worried did nothing to reassure her.

"Karma, I just heard." Her mother grabbed her in a fierce hug. "I'm so proud of you, sweeting."

KT looked questioningly at her sister, who ducked her head like she was guilty. What would Bijou be guilty about? She shook her head and awkwardly patted Lara's head. "Um. Great, Mom. Thanks."

Her mom took her by the shoulders. "When can I hear it?"

"Hear what?"

"Your concerto, sweeting. What else would I be talking about?"

"Concerto?" Her gaze flew to Bijou's, who grimaced.

"Your sister told me you were working on a masterpiece and that it was beyond anything she'd ever heard." Her mom went to the piano and began rifling through the scattered sheet music there. She lifted a sheet and began reading it, humming the notes as she went along.

Hands on her hips, KT faced her sister. "What the hell?"

Bijou stepped closer, her hand out imploringly. "Just go along with it. I have a plan."

"I had a plan, too," she whispered in a hiss.

"Your plan sucked."

"It did not."

Bijou took her arm and lowered her voice even more. "It wasn't working, KT. But if she thinks you're the next Beethoven, she's not going to force you to perform at a rock concert."

Okay, that was likely true, she had to admit. But still. She crossed her arms. "You tattled on me. You always had my back before."

At least Bijou had the grace to look guilty. "I was trying to save you."

"And yourself." She wanted her sister to deny it. When Bijou just grimaced, she felt a bone-deep sadness.

Her mother propped one of the sheets on the piano and settled on the bench. She squinted at the music and then began to pick out the notes. KT winced as her mom hit a wrong note, paused, and then corrected it. Her mom didn't even bat an eyelash. If KT had done that in front of anyone, even her family, she'd have died.

Her mom began to sing along, reading the words cold off the sheet. Lara's voice was huskier than KT's. Her mom was good, hitting all the right points even though this was her first time through.

Hearing her mom sing her song made her chest feel tight. KT closed her eyes and listened.

The music stopped, and she reopened her eyes to find her mother staring at her with tears streaming down her cheeks. "Karma, that's the most beautiful piece of music I've heard in a long time."

Stunned, not sure what to say, she shrugged and stuck her hands in her pockets.

"I didn't know. How could I not know you had

that" — Lara made a sweeping gesture to the sheet music — "in you?"

"KT has a good poker face," Chance's voice carried from the front.

She turned around and saw him leaning in the doorway, his arms crossed, and she felt oddly relieved to see him.

He must have sensed her tension, because he pushed off the wall and came directly to her and gave her a soft kiss, all the while holding her gaze. He ran his hand down her back, letting it rest on her hip. "What's going on here?"

"Bijou ratted out my music to Mom."

He raised his brow, glancing at her sister.

Bijou held her hand out. "I'm the rat. Nice to meet you."

Chance accepted her hand with a nod. "I'm sure it wasn't like that."

"No, it pretty much was," KT assured him.

"The heavens blessed you when they sent you a sister like Bijou," her mother said, standing up. "You should be thanking her."

She glared at the traitor. "Right."

"In any case," her mother continued, "it's good

that I'm aware of this new turn your career is taking. We're going to have to rethink the concert."

She perked up. "We are?"

"Of course, sweeting. This has a classical bent, and we do rock and roll. The audience will be confused." Her mother tapped a finger to her lips, thinking. "Maybe we can have you open with a piece of your concerto and then Bijou can follow with something that riffs off your music. Bijou, can you write a song based on KT's?"

Her sister looked panicked for a second before she schooled her expression. "Well, sure, but don't you think KT's music is inappropriate for this venue?"

"Good music is never inappropriate, sweeting."

Bijou turned to her, stricken, clearly at a loss for words.

Cold fear snaked around KT's heart so completely, she didn't have it in herself to rub her sister's mistake in her face. Not even Chance's firm hold was reassuring. She swallowed thickly and said, "Maybe I should skip the performance."

"Of course not, Karma. It's a family event."

Her mother looked at her like she was insane. "Or I suppose you could, but then Bijou won't be able to perform either."

"That's really not fair, Mother."

"You're thirty, sweeting, not twelve. You should know by now that life isn't fair."

She threw her arms in the air and began to pace. "I don't understand why you're doing this. I'm not like you people. How screwed up is it that you're annoyed with me because I didn't turn out like how you wanted me to?"

"I'm not annoyed," her mother said calmly. "I simply want to light a fire under your derriere."

"Oh, it's lit."

"It's worked well so far." She gestured to Chance. "You found love. You wrote an amazing piece of music. You're even teaching. Why would I back off now?"

KT gaped at her mother. Then she looked at Bijou. "This was your great idea?"

Bijou shrugged helplessly. "I didn't think she was so Machiavellian."

"You girls have always underestimated me," Lara said mildly.

Chance stepped forward. "Lara, maybe there's some other way for KT to contribute."

"Because Chance and I have plans next week during the concert," KT added.

Her mom frowned. "What sort of plans?"

Oh geez—what sort of plans would be major enough to deter her mother? "We're getting married," she heard herself say.

The silence in the room was profound.

She turned horrified eyes to Chance.

He looked surprised for an instant but then his poker face slipped back into place. He pulled her into his arms and touched her face, a nonverbal trust me. Then he turned to Lara. "We wanted it to be a surprise."

"It is that." Her mother came toward them, her arms outstretched. "Congratulation, sweetings. I'm so thrilled you found each other. I knew you were the man for my Karma when I met you, Chance. Your auras mingle so nicely."

KT met Chance's gaze over her mother's head. She couldn't tell how he felt about her lie. It was one thing telling everyone they were dating, but telling them they were getting married . . .

Lara frowned at them. "But what's this about getting married next week?"

"In Vegas." Chance smiled winningly at her mom. "It's my fault. I can't wait to make her mine."

Bijou stepped forward, arms crossed. "KT, you didn't tell me you were that serious."

She felt a pang of guilt for the hurt in her sister's eyes, but she reminded herself that Bijou ratted her out.

Before she could reply, her mom grabbed her hand and inspected her fingers. "Where's your ring, Karma?"

"We're still looking for the perfect one," Chance inserted quickly. "And you know how KT feels about shopping."

Yes, Bijou and Lara knew, but how did Chance? She looked at him, puzzled.

Lara shook her head. "This is so much to comprehend. Not only do we have a genius on our hands, but she's getting married. Wait until I tell Anson. And you two get it out of your head that you're getting married without family around you. We'll discuss that later. I can see you two want to be alone."

KT flushed at the wink her mom gave Chance. Fortunately, Lara took Bijou by the hand and led her out, closing the cottage door behind them.

KT faced Chance. "I'm so sorry."

"For what?"

"For getting you roped into a fake wedding." She grabbed her hair, the full weight of her actions coming down on her. "I don't know what happened."

"It's okay, KT." Chance took her hands in his and squeezed. "We'll draw it out until the concert is over and then it won't matter. You can break it off with me."

"Mom will think I'm crazy, letting you go." She thought she was crazy for considering it, too.

"You can tell her I left my dirty underwear all over the place, or that I snored."

"You don't snore."

He touched her cheek. "I like that you know that."

"What did I say?" KT smacked her forehead. "She's going to make me go dress shopping, and I get none of the fringe benefits of being engaged."

"What fringe benefits?"

"Like cake tasting."

"I think we can arrange cake for you." He tugged her closer and nuzzled her neck. "And other benefits."

She arched her neck to give him better access, sighing as her tension melted away. He had that effect on her. "How can we taste cake when we haven't even had a proper proposal?"

"Are you fishing?" he murmured against her skin.

She pouted. "No."

Lifting his head, he traced her lower lip with his finger, a hint of a smile lightening his expression. "You may deny it, but you're a closet romantic. Trust me, you'll get your cake and eat it, too."

She tugged him closer by his belt loops. "I'd like something spicy now instead of sweet."

"That I can do." He hiked her over his shoulder, groaning dramatically. "Although maybe you shouldn't be eating more cake."

Laughing, she smacked his butt as he carried her to her bedroom. And then they were too busy to laugh for a long time.

Chapter Fourteen

*W*ILL DIDN'T LOOK surprised to see Bijou waiting alone.

"I forgot to bring KT," she said, facing him. "But I had a good reason."

"Aliens abducted her?"

"Therapists aren't supposed to be sarcastic."

"You told me you weren't here for therapy." He smiled crookedly at her.

"I'm not." She strode into his office and began to pace. "Do you think I'm selfish?"

"We're all selfish." He closed the door. "We need to be to a certain extent because if we don't make ourselves happy, no one around us will be happy either."

"Yes, but I've been overly focused on myself." She remembered the betrayed look on her sister's face and winced. "I need to change that."

"What happened that's causing you to feel this way?"

She stopped pacing and faced him, hands on her hips. "You're being a shrink again."

He smiled unapologetically. "It's what I do."

"I don't need a shrink. I need a friend."

Will reached for his coat and took her hand. "Let's go for a walk, then."

"You have no problem being my friend?" she asked, trying not to get distracted by the feel of his calloused fingertips rasping her skin. "And before you ask me if I have problems with my friends, the answer is no. It's just that men always assume it means more."

"I wouldn't assume anything with you, Bijou." Flashing her a grin, he squeezed her hand as he guided her out of his office and onto the street. "Let's take the trolley to the Ferry Building. We won't find chocolate croissants as delicious as that café you took me to in Laurel Heights, but I'm sure we'll find something that we like."

She had something she liked right next to her. "You're too attractive for your own good."

"So you say." The trolley pulled up to the stop just as they reached it. Will paid for their tickets and then they stood next to each other, holding onto the same pole. "Out of curiosity, why didn't KT come today?"

"I really did forget to tell her about the appointment. I intended to drag her to the session but things happened." She made a face. "It might be more accurate to say that I tattled on her to Mom and then it all went to crap."

He chuckled. "My little sister used to tattle on me all the time. Drove me crazy."

How come she didn't know he had a little sister? It seemed like something she should know. See — she really was selfish and focused on herself. "We always talk about me, don't we?"

"I could hardly charge people to talk about myself."

She shook her head. "It's a good thing you haven't been charging me. Tell me about your family. Where does your sister live?"

"Portland, Oregon, but something's bothering you and I want to hear what it is."

The trolley jerked to a stop. Before Bijou could brace herself, she flew into him.

Will caught her by her waist. They looked into each other's eyes. Bijou held her breath, afraid of stirring the sudden tension between them, one way or the other.

His fingers tightened on her waist. "I don't like to see you unhappy," he said softly. "Tell me what happened."

She sighed and let go. "I overheard KT playing the most beautiful classical music ever."

"That's saying something."

"You don't even know." She looked him in the eye. "She composed it."

"I didn't realize she composed classical music."

"Neither did I." She frowned. "It's something I should have known. I'm her sister. We're close, and I had no clue."

He held her steady as the bus stopped again. "Is that why you think you're selfish?"

"I think I'm selfish because I told Lara about KT's music to benefit myself."

His brow furrowed. "I don't understand how it could benefit you."

"Classical music has no place at a rock concert. If KT goes classical, Mom would stop insisting that KT has to perform or I can't." She sighed.

"I take it Lara didn't see it the same way."

"Hardly."

"This is our stop," he said, nodding toward the exit. Still holding her hand, they walked in silence into the Ferry Building.

It was midday, but the market inside was always busy. Will led the way through the throng of people to a little organic bakery and produce stand. He bought them a fruit tart to share, and they took it outside to a bench on the pier.

She tilted her head back, eyes closed, and let the sunlight warm her. Something about the rays on her reminded her of KT's music. "You should have heard KT play her music. It was powerful. Amazing. You'd understand, being a musician."

"I'm a therapist, really."

She opened her eyes and looked at him. He looked like he could step on stage and have women throwing underwear at him. "Right. Not buying it."

Grinning, he handed her a piece of the tart. "You're good for my ego."

She looked at the tart in her hand. "I didn't work out today."

"Live on the wild side, Bijou. A couple bites

185

of tart won't hurt you." He handed her his water bottle.

She took it and sipped, conscious of the intimacy of sharing it. She passed it back to him. "I wish you could hear KT's concerto. It was genius. KT always showed a little genius, but she'd never let on this much talent. That music was pure love and longing and strength."

"It inspired you."

"Yes." She angled toward him; her knees touched his. "I feel a buzzing inside me, an urge to write something down."

He brushed a strand of her hair away from her face. "You feel your magic resurfacing?"

She definitely felt something sizzling inside right now, but she was pretty sure it was because of him rather than her creative juices. "I don't know that I'd go that far."

"Have you tried?"

Her breath froze in her gorge at the thought. "No."

"Want to try now?"

"No."

He laughed, caressing her hand. "At the risk

of sounding like a shrink, you know you're going to have to attempt to write a song again at some point."

"Sooner as opposed to later." She cleared her throat to dislodge the fear settling there. "Mom wants me to write a song that segues from KT's concerto to the rest of the concert."

"That's powerful motivation to get over your block."

She turned to him. "What if I don't?"

"You will," he replied with unwavering faith.

It wasn't lip service—he meant it. She felt his confidence all the way to her core, and the way he held her hand only deepened the feeling of conviction.

She stared at their clasped hands. She'd never felt so connected to a man. What she'd felt for Brice didn't even come close.

Which terrified her because if Brice wielded so much power over her, what havoc could Will wreak?

Bijou thought of the love she'd seen on her sister's face when Chance walked in, and a shadowed part of her heart puckered in jealousy. "KT is engaged," she heard herself say.

"To someone she's been seeing a while?"

"Not at all. She didn't tell me she was engaged, either. KT's always been private, but she's never hid things from me."

Will ran a soothing hand down her hair, resting on her shoulder. "You feel hurt."

"It just seems like such powerful music is born out of love." She angled to face him. "I guess I just expected her to tell me if she'd fallen in love."

"Did you tell her when you fell in love?"

"I told the world." She winced, thinking of her song. "Did you, or were you private?"

"I don't hide my feelings, Bijou." He tilted her head up and lowered his lips to hers. His kiss tasted like sweet, dark berries and promises. He took his time, like she was a treat to be savored just like the tart they'd shared.

Without thought, she hitched her leg over his and gripped his lapels to pull herself closer.

His left arm stole around her waist, holding her to him. He took his time, kissing her with slow deliberation, a little tongue, a little playful—a lot hot. He tasted her like he had all the time in the world, and she was the only thing he was interested in.

Humming, she arched into him, wishing his hand would do its own exploring. She lifted her mouth from his. "You don't like anyone now, do you?"

"Actually, there's someone I do like." He brushed his lips on hers.

There was no mistaking his meaning, and she gave in to the delicious feel of his mouth. But she forced herself to say, "I won't date musicians."

"I'm a therapist," he said, sitting back but not letting go of her. "I just happen to play at times, too. And it seems like you'd want someone who shares your interests."

"You don't know much about me, except that I have crazy parents and am selfish. The only thing we share is lust."

He rubbed her palm with his thumb. "So we're in lust, but not in like?"

She shivered at his touch, still wishing his hands were all over her despite herself. "Isn't that what we are?"

"You know it's not." He tugged her over, until

she sat straddled on his lap facing him.

Bijou swallowed thickly, her heart pounding in excitement. He'd barely touched her and already she was jumping out of her skin. "I don't date bad boys anymore."

Smiling wickedly, Will wrapped his fingers in her hair. "I'm all good, Bijou."

He pulled her head down to kiss her, slowly, giving her time to protest.

But she wanted it just as much as he did. He knew it, and—worse—she did, too. She couldn't back away even if he gave her the space. The kiss was necessary.

It was an education.

No one had ever truly kissed her before. What Brice called affection was like a schoolboy's floundering. She didn't have words for how deep Will's kiss went.

She lifted her head, very aware of his arousal pressing between her legs, but she did nothing to encourage it. Instead, she tried to catch her breath and decide what to do.

He ran a hand over her hip. "You're thinking."

"You're giving me a lot to ponder."

"Sometimes you have to feel, not think."

She arched her brow. "This from a therapist?"

"There's a balance in things." He drew her closer. "Wasn't that the least bit compelling?"

"It definitely was, but I'm not sure how far I should be compelled."

"Maybe you can be compelled into going out with me Friday night. A friend has a gig. I said I'd stop by."

"Okay." She started to slide off him, the words feel, don't think repeating in her head to the rhythm of KT's concerto.

He stopped her with a hand on her thigh. "Bijou?"

"Yes?"

"Think about being in like."

Swallowing a sudden lump of fear, she nodded. She wasn't sure she'd be able to think about anything else.

Chapter Fifteen

CHANCE WALKED INTO the morning room, as Elise called it. "Have you seen Ante—"

But he didn't need to finish his sentence because his pig sat very properly at Elise's feet, snout in the air, seemingly waiting patiently.

"There you are, darling." Elise cut a piece of French toast from her plate and fed it straight off the fork to the little porker. "I hope you don't mind that we didn't wait for you for breakfast. Give Celeste a call, and she'll bring you a fresh batch."

He took a cup from the sideboard, giving his porcine buddy a pointed look. "You're going to have to do an extra workout today, you know."

Ante Up turned away, giving his full, adoring attention to Elise.

"Traitor." Shaking his head, Chance sat across from Elise. His phone buzzed, but he silenced it when he saw it was just Tiffany Woods.

She studied him, a faint frown lining her forehead. "You seem different, darling."

"Different?" he asked, sipping the coffee.

"The past weeks you've been jittery with nervous energy. You seem more settled this morning." She raised her brow. "Any particular reason?"

He smiled faintly. "I have a feeling you already know exactly what's going on."

She fed the pig another bite. "Well, Lara Taylor has lived next door to me for decades. It's obvious we'd be friends."

Actually, it wasn't obvious at all. Elise oozed society and refinement from every pore. Lara was more earthly. From what he'd seen at Harvard, old money and new didn't usually mix. In fact, as a "poor" student, he'd been better received by the parents of the girls he'd dated. Overcoming your background was in fashion, he guessed.

But then Elise was different than the typical society matron. It stood to reason since Scott was so down-to-earth.

Elise gave him a look. "Are you going to tell me what's going on between you and Karma, or do I have to hold your pig hostage?"

"That wouldn't be a feat. He has Stockholm syndrome already."

Ante Up just continued to look at her adoringly.

Chance shook his head. Then he faced Elise. "KT and I are engaged."

"Congratulations, darling." She didn't sound the least bit surprised. "Karma is a lovely girl; the rare breed who doesn't realize how wonderful and talented she is. I've always thought it'd take a special man to allow her the space to find herself, but I couldn't have picked a better man for her myself. Lara is beside herself with happiness."

He nodded, not sure how he felt. Guilty about the ruse, because he hated deceiving Elise. Oddly, he also felt somehow satisfied about the engagement. His head kept reminding him it was fake, but his heart dared him to believe otherwise.

"You don't look certain, Chance." Elise frowned. "Are you having cold feet already?"

Normally he wouldn't have even considered confessing. If you wanted to bluff, you had to commit yourself to it. You didn't show your hand.

But the way Elise stared at him, with concern

195

and affection, reminded him of his mom. He hadn't had anyone care like that about him in a long time.

So he found himself saying, "Can I make a confession about my relationship with KT?"

"Being adventurous between the sheets is nothing to be ashamed of."

He felt his face flush. "Not that type of confession."

"A pity."

"We're not really dating."

Elise blinked. "And yet you're engaged?"

"It started out pretend. I needed someone to help me keep that headhunter at bay, and KT needed to date someone to distract her mom. So we entered a partnership of sorts."

"And this somehow led to a proposal?"

"Actually, I haven't proposed yet."

Elise frowned. "You sound like you plan to."

He thought about the ring he'd seen in the jewelry store a few blocks away and nodded. "This afternoon."

Shaking her head, she set her fork down. "Let me get this straight. You and KT have been dating for the past couple weeks?"

"Yes."

"You've kissed?"

At every opportunity. He nodded.

Elise raised a brow. "You've been intimate?"

Like he was going to admit that to Scott's mom. He squirmed in his chair.

"Don't answer that. I can tell by the look on your face." She gave him a knowingly look. "Given all the facts, your relationship doesn't seem very pretend, does it?"

"Not when you put it that way."

"Do you know what I think?"

"Do I want to know?" he asked with an amused smile.

"I think you found your port," she said as though he hadn't spoken. "I think you're smart enough to realize a good thing when you see one. You came here searching, and you've found part of what you're looking for. You're too smart a man to let that go. If you were upset about getting married to KT, you'd be pacing right now, trying to climb out of the hole you dug instead of thinking about proposing to her."

True—all of it.

Elise scratched Ante Up behind his ear. "You need to ask yourself what you want, Chance."

KT. The answer was loud and clear. He wanted to find a place and live with her and her enormous piano, and come home from whatever strange hours his job had to find her playing her music. He wanted to kiss her whenever he wanted and know that she'd always be next to him, holding his hand, backing him up even when it put him out of his comfort zone.

He stood up. "Do you mind keeping an eye on Ante Up this afternoon?"

"Of course not." She smiled fondly at the pig. "I'll take him to be groomed. How do you feel about a pedicure, darling?" she asked the pig.

Ante Up snorted enthusiastically, standing up.

"There you go." Elise smiled at Chance. "Go ahead and do what you need, darling. We'll be here."

He leaned down to kiss her cheek. "Thank you, Elise."

Cupping his cheek, she smiled at him. "I should thank you, Chance."

"What for?"

"For letting me mother you."

"How about if we make a deal?" He took her hand. "I'll let you mother me all you want."

"This deal seems awfully one-sided. What do you get out of it?"

"I think that'd be obvious. Everything." He kissed her cheek.

She touched his face. "When you put it that way, how can I refuse?"

**His first stop was Romantic Notions. A man had to have his priorities straight.

The shop lady, Olivia, remembered him. She picked out what she assured him was the perfect set for KT. He had to agree—it was a deep emerald silk with strategically placed black lace that'd look spectacular on her.

His second stop went just as smoothly, until he exited the jewelry store and bumped into someone. He started to apologize when he realized the "someone" was actually Tiffany Woods.

"Chance," she exclaimed brightly. "What a surprise."

If by surprise she really meant creepy. "What are you doing here?"

"A little shopping on my break."

He looked pointedly at the lack of bags in her hand.

Her lips thinned as she noted the jewelry store's sign. Then she nodded at the tiny Romantic Notions bag in his hand. "Shopping for your girlfriend?" she said as if the idea was distasteful.

"My fiancée actually," he corrected, touching his pocket where the ring he'd bought for KT was. He'd seen it in the window one time when he'd walked by, and it reminded him of her: simple, bold, and shiny.

An awkward silence stretched over the conversation. He glanced at Tiffany, shocked to see bereft loneliness on every line of her face.

But then her expression turned to stone, and she coolly said, "Fiancée."

"You met her a couple weeks ago." Maybe he'd imagined her loneliness? Now she just looked like she wanted to carve KT's heart out.

Tiffany hiked her behemoth purse up into the crook of her arm, her tone frigid. "I've been trying to contact you regarding the quantitative analyst position. I see why you've been so unavailable."

Wait a minute—she only ever called him to ask him out. He wanted to point that out but then he remembered he didn't have a way to contact Roger Leif directly.

Resisting the urge to curse, instead he said, "I'm available whenever Roger is free to meet."

"I'll let him know." She ran a hand through her hair, giving him a knowing look. "But I'm sure you and I can work out the details on our own. Give me call when you're ready, Chance."

He wasn't sure he'd ever be ready. Except he'd done some research into other companies and no one seemed to be hiring except for Paragon.

What he needed to do was bypass the middleman and contact Roger Leif directly.

Later. Shaking off the encounter, he pulled out his phone to text KT. Coming over.

Her response was instant: I'm not decent.

He grinned and replied: Good. See you in 5.

She was waiting at her cottage door for him,

her long, lean body propped in the doorway. As he approached, a smile lit her face.

He suddenly knew without a doubt that he wanted to make that smile happen for the rest of his life. He walked up to her and kissed those lips with as much feeling as he'd ever felt.

"Take this," he said, handing her the little burgundy lingerie bag.

"What is it?" She shook it.

"A present for me." Then he got down on one knee.

She blinked at him; the bag dropping from her fingertips. "What are you doing?"

"Giving you your present." He took out of the small box from his jacket pocket, opened it, and extracted the ring.

KT swallowed audibly. "I hope that's a pretend rock."

"No." He took her hand and kissed her ring finger.

"You should have gotten me a ring out of a bubblegum machine."

"You deserve more than that." Then he looked up into her eyes as he slid the ring on her finger. It fit perfectly, but then he knew it would. "I wanted to do it right."

She stared at her hand, her eyes wide. "This is —"

"What?"

She shook her head and met his gaze helplessly. "This doesn't feel pretend."

He heard the panic in her tone, and his heart dipped in disappointment that she wasn't as excited about this as he was. His gut told him he was rushing the game, that he needed to let this hand play out more before he won.

So he stood and tried to smile carelessly. "It has to look real for your mom to believe it. Don't worry, KT. We're just the way we were before."

"Whew." She relaxed visibly, looking down at her ring. "For a moment, I thought you'd lost your mind."

He smiled, knowing it wasn't his mind that he'd lost.

Chapter Sixteen

$\mathcal{K}$T'S FINGERS GLIDED over the piano keys distractedly as she wondered what to teach Ashley today. Their last couple lessons had been a revelation—the kid had serious talent. She still didn't like teaching, but at least the teenager's skill made it interesting.

"I wondered who was in here."

She turned around, stopping, and saw Lola leaning in the doorway.

The blonde gestured with her hand. "Don't stop playing. It was lovely."

She shrugged, self-conscious. To divert Lola's attention, she asked, "Is the little monster here yet?"

"Not yet." Lola grinned and walked into the room. "She's endeared herself to you that much, huh?"

"She's precious." KT made a face. Truth of the matter was she liked Ashley. Not that she'd ever admit that. "We're making headway though. I didn't threaten her last time, so that's something."

Lola chuckled. "I've had one or two of those. I'm always grateful my stepdaughter is so sweet."

She imagined being in charge of a child. Chance was in the picture holding her hand as she looked at a mutated version of the two of them.

She shook the oddly compelling image out of her mind.

"Is that an engagement ring?" Lola screeched, grabbing her hand.

KT blinked in surprise.

"You've been holding out, woman." Still holding her hand, Lola raised her voice. "Gwen, get your booty in here!"

Gwen came rushing in. "What's wrong?"

"KT got engaged"—Lola held up the evidence—"and didn't tell us."

Gasping, Gwen grabbed KT in a hug. "That's so wonderful. Congratulations!"

"Who is he?" Lola asked KT before turning to Gwen. "Do you see this ring? It's awesome."

Gwen bent over KT's hand. "It reminds me of a ring my grandmother had. It's like a tiger's eye."

"I love it, because it's different. I bet he took care finding the perfect ring." Lola arched her brow. "This man did good. You should keep him."

Overwhelmed, KT just nodded. "I really want to."

"Of course you do." Gwen patted her shoulder. "You said yes to him, after all."

Well, she hadn't, because they didn't have a real proposal, but she would have. She thought she might say yes to anything he asked.

A freaky thought if there ever was one.

"What's going on?"

The three of them looked to the doorway to see a confused Ashley standing there.

KT retracted her hand from the women's. "Gwen and Lola were just consoling me because I told them how you see it as your mission to torment me."

"Yeah, right." The girl rolled her eyes, but there was a tiny hint of a smile at her lips. "More like they should be consoling me. I mean, come on, couldn't you guys find a real teacher for me?"

Grinning, Gwen walked up to the girl and patted her arm. "I'll try to do better next time."

Ashley snorted. "The bar is low, so there's that."

"I think you're precious, too," KT crooned with a saccharine smile.

Lola laughed and slung her arm around Gwen's shoulders. "It's a love match if I ever saw one."

"It's something," Gwen said, shaking her head as they left the room.

The kid strode to the piano bench and dropped her backpack. "Are you going to hog up the whole bench, or do I get to sit, too?"

"At least you didn't say my ass is fat." KT moved over, setting some sheet music on the stand in front of them.

Ashley groaned.

"Get over it, kid." She opened the songbook and creased the first page so it'd stay open. "Reading is fundamental."

"I don't understand why I need to read." She glared at music. "I just want to make songs."

"Don't look at Erik Satie's 'Gymnopédie' that way, and you don't make sense. How can you make music if you can't write it down?"

"I'll remember it all in my head."

KT snorted. "Good decision. And then what?" Ashley frowned. "What do you mean?"

"What's your purpose?" KT heard herself ask. Mentally, she smacked herself for sounding like Chance, but she also knew without a doubt Ashley had a purpose, and her purpose was to play the piano.

"You sound like a self-help guru," the kid grumbled. "I just want to play."

"I don't know where you come from but based on the fact that you're here playing this crappy piano"—KT waved dismissively at the upright—"means that you don't have rich parents."

The teenager sneered, crossing her arms. "Way to figure that out, Sherlock."

"No." She took the kid's arms and uncrossed them. "Right now we're not going to play games. This is me and you, being real, and I'm telling you you're good. I've only ever met one other person who had such an affinity for the piano."

"Who?" Ashley asked, seemingly despite herself.

"Me." KT grinned. Then she sobered. "If you worked on your technique and learned to read music, you could do anything you wanted. Compose, sell jingles, or play in a bar. Whatever. This is your ticket out into the world."

Ashley frowned. "Was piano your ticket out?"

KT sat back. "We're not talking about me."

"We kind of are," the kid mumbled.

Yeah, but she didn't come out of the slums, or wherever Ashley lived. She was a rock princess with a cushy lifestyle. She had all the opportunities in the world, and what was she doing? Wasting them.

Her mother's voice spoke in her mind: It's a crime not to realize your full potential, Karma.

Then she heard Chance ask her: What's your purpose?

Guilt made her scowl. "Just play the frickin' song, Spike."

Still griping under her breath, the girl squinted at the music and began to haltingly play.

They'd worked on sight-reading the last couple lessons. Ashley was vastly improved, but she was still fighting against it and it showed.

"Stop," KT said after a particularly painful section. "You're playing it all wrong, which is impressive considering you're playing Satie, and his music is so loose. Look at the notes. It doesn't say staccato."

Ashley glared at her. "If you're so great, you play it."

"Fine." She pushed the girl over with her hip and played the song the way Satie meant it to be.

She'd always loved Satie and the simple beauty of his work. She closed her eyes and let the music play through her. "The thing about learning to read music is that it opens doors in your mind. You can listen to someone's rendition of a song, but then you're going to think of the song the way that person does. It's like regurgitating someone else's ideas.

"But if you can read, you can interpret for yourself." KT let herself go free, doing her own version of the Gymnopédie. "You develop your own opinions and thoughts. You get ideas. It's knowledge, and knowledge is power."

She stopped playing and turned to Ashley.

There was shocked amazement on the kid's face. She stared at KT like she'd never seen her before.

Frowning, KT tried not to squirm uncomfortably. "Why are you staring at me like that?"

Ashley shook her head. "I've never heard you play. That was . . ."

"What?" she asked warily.

"Something I want to do." Ashley faced the sheet music, her mouth set in a determined line.

KT gaped at the girl, not sure what to say. She was happy when the teenager started to play again so there was no need to say anything.

Chapter Seventeen

THE TEXT CAME in as Chance was putting his shoes on for a run. He looked at his phone, excited that it might be KT, but he immediately deflated when he saw who it was from. "Aw hell."

Ante Up stopped exploring the bedroom and looked up at him, his snout wiggling inquisitively.

Chance held his phone up. "It's Tiffany Woods. She's invited me to attend a cocktail party tonight that Leif is putting on."

The pig jerked his head with a snort.

"I know I was the one who emailed her to say I hoped we could work something out, but I meant professionally."

Ante stared at him like he was an idiot.

Chance pointed at the oinker. "Don't say a word."

He swore the pig rolled its eyes.

"I want that job. I need to connect with Roger Leif, and this cocktail party is my chance." He watched the pig duck his head under a shirt Chance had dropped on the ground. "That's what I think, too. You know what I need to do?"

Ante Up peeked out.

"Take KT with me." He pulled a clean shirt on and raked his fingers through his hair. "Unless you want to come along?"

The pig snarfled, nestling into the shirt.

"I didn't think so, and I can't really blame you." He scratched the little fellow behind the ears and went to see KT.

When he arrived at her carriage house, he stuck his ear to the door and listened.

The door jerked open, and an annoyed looking KT stood glaring at him. "What the hell, Nolan?"

"You can't blame me for trying," he said, easing his arms around her waist and pulling her into him. "It's like searching for a little heaven on earth."

She thawed a little, her scowl becoming more like a pout. "What are you doing? There's no one here to see you do this, you know."

"I'm being careful, just in case someone's spying on us," he lied. He grazed his lips against hers and then nuzzled her neck.

She sighed. "You're being opportunistic."

"Yes."

"I guess I don't mind." She wound her arms around his neck.

"You guess?" he murmured, kissing the spot on her neck that made her shiver.

"Do you want a written invitation, or are you going to kiss me, damn it?"

He grinned, wrapping his hand in her long hair and tugging her head back. "Say pretty please."

Her gorgeous eyes narrowed.

Chuckling, he kissed her and then his amusement faded into something powerful and urgent. He pressed her against the door, his mouth devouring her like she was the oasis he'd spent years searching for.

She murmured against his lips, "Are you still acting in case someone's watching?"

"No, this is just all for your benefit. Mine, too, but mostly yours at the moment." He kissed her again, his hand slipping under her top to feel her warm, soft skin and the swell of her breast.

She sighed. "If you just came here to make out, maybe we should take this inside."

"Actually, I came here to see if you were free to go to a cocktail party tonight." He massaged the base of her neck. "It's a business opportunity, and I need to be there."

"Which means the cannibal will be there," she surmised.

"Right."

KT smirked. "So you need me to protect you?"

"Hell yes. I'm not proud."

"I think my suit of armor is out being cleaned."

"Damn." He brushed back her hair. "You think you can find a dress to wear instead?"

She winced. "I hate social gatherings."

"I know." He stared at her steadily, wanting her to go. He realized it wasn't just because of Tiffany but because he wanted her to be with him.

That was something to think about later. For now, he didn't want to coerce her into a situation she didn't want to be in. "It's okay if you don't go. I understand."

"No, I'll go with you." She sighed. "It's our deal."

"I don't want you to go because you feel it's your duty."

At first he didn't think she was going to respond but then she bit her lip, shrugged, and said, "I'll go with you so just shut up about it."

"You're so enthusiastic," he joked.

She pushed him away. "Get lost. I need to dig out my armor."

"Pick you up at seven?"

"I'll be here with bells on," she said sarcastically, stepping back into her cottage.

He smiled all the way back to his room.

**She was waiting for him at exactly seven, standing on her stoop, tapping her foot impatiently. She wore head-to-toe black, wrapped tightly in a shawl that covered her down to her hips, and an expression like she was headed toward her last meal.

"I think I didn't mention that it's not a wake," he said, walking up to her and kissing her cheek.

She glared at him. "I wore makeup for you."

He looked at her face. She had a little shimmer on her eyelids and her lashes looked thick and long. Her lips glistened pink, inviting. He wanted to kiss the color off. "You look just as beautiful as usual."

She frowned. "You can't tell? You mean I subjected myself to my sister's torture for an hour for nothing?"

"You're always beautiful." He took her arm. "The car's out front."

"Where's Ante Up?" she asked as they strolled through the garden out front.

"With Elise."

"How did you get Elise Carrington-Wright to babysit a pig?"

"No one can withstand that little porker's charm." He glanced at her. "He and I are a lot alike."

She snorted.

Scott had left him his car to use while he was on his honeymoon. He opened the door for KT and then went around to get in. He could tell KT was nervous, so as soon as he pulled away from the curb, he took her hand and began to tell her about the man they were meeting tonight. By the time they arrived, she'd relaxed, only to tense up again as they reached the threshold.

Chance turned to her before ringing the bell and lifted her chin. "Thank you for stepping out of your comfort zone and doing this."

"You're so making this up to me."

Her eyes flashed defiantly despite her nerves, and his heart swelled with emotion for her. He kissed her temple and said, "How about the first thing we do is get you a glass of wine?"

"Whiskey, and you're on." She reached forward and pressed the ringer.

The door opened, revealing Leif. Their host smiled, taking Chance's hand and clapping his arm. "I was just talking about you, Chance. Come in. Glad you could make it."

"Thanks for inviting me," he replied stepping inside.

But Roger's attention was already on KT. "Well, hello there. I'm Roger Leif."

Lips set in a determined downturn, KT shook his hand. "KT," she said simply.

"Can I take your wrap?"

For a moment, Chance didn't think she'd give it up, but then she sighed with resignation and handed it over.

His jaw dropped. The back half was missing.

Roger was no less impressed. In fact, Chance wanted to take the shawl back to get the guy's lecherous eyes off his girlfriend.

Instead, he smoothly stepped in front of her, blocking her from the man. "Which way to the bar?"

"Right in the living room." Roger pointed the way, then craned his neck to look at KT. "I hope to see you more later."

She rolled her eyes and strode in the direction Roger indicated. Once they were clear, she turned around with a glare. "I can feel you staring."

"I can't help it." Her dress was a black sheath, simple, with the tiniest straps at the shoulders. In the front it scooped low, but it was all party in the back, dipping low to the top of her ass. "It's nice."

"It's Bijou's."

"Remind me to thank your sister when I see her next." He put his tongue back in his mouth and slipped an arm around her waist. "And it's more like half a dress, though, for the record I'm not complaining."

She glanced at him, suspicious.

"You look amazing. Really, truly amazing." He brushed a hand down her spine, gratified at her shiver. "No bra, right?"

She looked at him like he was crazy. "That would have been like insult to injury."

"You. Me. This dress in a pile on the floor." He pushed her hair over her shoulder and kissed her there. "Later."

"As if I needed more incentive to get this over with." She took his hand. "Don't look now, but I think that's your cannibal over there, and she's watching us."

He glanced over where KT indicated. Sure enough, Tiffany watched him with irritation.

"Don't leave me. She looks like she'd happily take me out if she got me alone." KT used her thumb to wipe what he supposed was lipstick from his mouth. "What did you do to her to get her so worked up?"

"I wish I knew so I could be careful not to do it again."

"I can't really blame her. You're some serious catnip, Nolan." She patted his chest. "Where's that whiskey you promised me?"

They walked to the bar, and the bartender gave them hefty triple pours. He sipped his, watching KT knock hers back and then ask for another. He smiled. "Am I going to have to carry you home?"

She shook her head as she took a more modest sip. "Can't stand crowds and people staring at me."

Of course she couldn't. He felt a swell of love for her, that she willingly put herself through this for him. He lifted her hand and kissed her fingers right below his ring. "Thank you."

Her brow wrinkled, and she opened her mouth to speak but then Roger and another couple were suddenly descending on them.

"Chance," Roger said, slapping his shoulder again. "This is Steve Hall and his wife Leslie. Steve's in finance, too. Chance is the poker player I was telling you about."

"Good to meet you, Chance." Steve smiled at him warmly. "Though I wish I'd met you before Roger. He's been bragging about what a find you are."

Aware KT had moved to stand a little behind him, Chance shook the man's hand, instantly liking his firm grip and no-nonsense gaze. "I'll have to remind him of that when we enter negotiations."

They all laughed, and Chance took that moment to face Leif. "Roger, do you have a card on you? I had some ideas regarding that tech company we discussed at Scott's wedding."

"Of course." Leif pulled out a card from his pocket. "It has my private number on it."

Score. Relief flooded over him. Maybe the situation was redeemable. "Excellent. I'll call you."

Steve's wife Leslie suddenly squinted at KT and said, "Aren't you Anson and Lara's daughter, Karma?"

He felt her freeze next to him. His instinct was to rescue her; he was about to pull her away, but she smiled stiffly and said, "I look a lot like her, don't I?"

Leslie smiled. "You do. You must get asked that a lot."

"It's better than being mistaken for Lindsay Lohan."

There was still tension at the edges of her mouth, so he took her hand. "If you'll excuse us, this is our song, and my girl's promised me a dance."

"That's so romantic." Leslie looked at him like he was a prince. "I need to have Steve take pointers from you. We'll arrange it later."

He flashed a smile and led KT away.

"There's no dance floor," she murmured as she downed the rest of her whiskey, handing the glass to a passing waiter.

"No, but there's open space here." He whirled her into his arms and kissed her, partly to calm her but mostly because he couldn't help himself. He moved her in time to the music. "This is Cole Porter."

"Yeah."

"My parents used to dance to Cole Porter." He waited for the usual feeling of loss that accompanied thoughts of his family. He felt it, but it was bearable with KT in his arms. "Mom used to sing the words to Dad as they danced."

"That's sweet." Under her breath, she hummed along with it.

He held her close, his eyes shut, knowing what his dad must have felt like.

Then the song changed, and KT stiffened.

"What's wrong?" he asked.

She shook her head. "It's just weird."

"Dancing with me?"

"Yeah." She rolled her eyes. "But to this song.

I wrote it."

He didn't have to listen long to know she wasn't singing it. "The recording isn't yours."

"Of course not. I told you I don't sing."

"I still think you should consider it. You have an amazing voice."

"I don't want to discuss this."

"Now isn't the time," he agreed. "But I still think going indie is a good solution for you."

She sighed. "You're not going to let this go, are you?"

"It's a smart, out-of-the-box option that'll get your music out in the public, without you having to ever show your face. You can even build your mystique into the marketing and turn your aversion to appearing publicly into an asset. You'd make yourself exclusive."

"Maybe," she said reluctantly, not sounding convinced.

"You'd never have to leave your cottage," he said with a wry grin. Then he sobered. "Think about it KT. You'd be playing by your own rules. You'd win."

"Winning is important to you."

"Everyone wants to win." He lifted her chin. "There's no reason you can't have everything you want, KT."

She didn't look like she believed him, and that broke his heart. Then she stepped out of his arms. "I'm getting a whiskey. Want something?"

"I want you to play the piano for me," he said, pulling her back.

"No." She gave him a withering look.

"Play me for it," he suggested in a sudden flash of brilliance. "Strip poker, winner takes all."

Her gaze narrowed. "What happens when I win?"

"You can have whatever you want." He looked her in the eye. "But if I win, you play the piano for me. Something you wrote."

She swallowed audibly. Then she nodded grimly, as if she was making a pact with the devil. "Fine."

"Let's go."

"Wait." She dug her heels in. "What about Leif and the cannibal?"

"He saw me, and I got his card. I'll give him a call tomorrow." Some things were more important, and KT was one of those things. He led her through the crowd and out of the house.

He'd expected the whiskey to hit her by the time they arrived at her place, but the only noticeable sign of intoxication was her volume level and her unsteady steps, though he wondered how much of that was just the unfamiliar heels she had on.

At the door, she opened her purse, looking for her keys. "Damn it."

He smiled as she kicked off her shoes and dumped them on the welcome mat. Sighing in relief, she unlocked the door and sauntered in. "You up for a nightcap?"

"I'm going to head out."

"What about our game?"

No one else would have suspected she was tipsy, but he could tell because he knew her. That knowledge made him feel honored, protective, like he was trusted with a precious treasure. "We're going to play tomorrow, when you're cold sober."

She pouted, waving a hand up and down her body. "And you're leaving before you get some of this?"

She was adorable. He bit his lip to keep from grinning, knowing she wouldn't appreciate his humor or being called adorable. Walking up to her, he slid his arms around her waist and pulled her to him. "That will be mine tomorrow, after you play the piano for me."

"In your dreams." She wiggled out of his arms. "Bring your piggy tomorrow. I want a witness when I cream you."

"Yes, ma'am." He tugged her back for a kiss and then grinned all the way home.

Chapter Eighteen

*W*HAT HAD SHE done?

KT paced in front of her piano, her anxiety growing by the hour as it got later. She checked the time. When was Chance coming over?

What had she promised?

She gripped her hair and growled. In the sober light of day, she saw how foolish she'd been. Agreeing to a challenge by, basically, a professional poker player? She was going to lose.

Part of her wanted to break out the whiskey again. He said he wanted her sober, but if she wasn't he'd probably still force her to play, and if she were a little sauced . . . Well, she'd have an excuse for screwing up.

She walked into the kitchen and pulled out her whiskey from the bottom shelf. Uncorking the top, she lifted it to swig out of the bottle —

And set it back down.

She couldn't do it. He'd be disappointed in

her, and that'd make her even more miserable.

She got her phone out and called him for the fifth time that evening. Just like every other time, his voicemail picked up. "How dare you not answer your phone," she yelled at him. "When the hell are you coming here for this game? You're a bastard for drawing it out like this. I take back all the nice things I've ever thought about you."

She hung up. Then she called him again and added, "And you better not bring your pig to strip poker. How could you even agree to such an indecent thing?"

Ending the call, she tossed her phone onto the couch and paced some more.

Fifteen minutes later, there was a knock on her door. She recognized the rapping as Chance's.

Her heart flopped in her chest. Usually it was because of Chance, but this time she was positive it had to be nerves. Exhaling loudly, she stomped to the door and glared as she opened it.

He stood on her stoop, an ever-ready grin curving his delicious lips. His hair was damp, and he wore a T-shirt and jeans with flip-flops. He looked hot, damn him.

"Hello, Karma," he said in his dark honey voice, kissing her lips softly as he walked inside. "I hope you're ready to play the piano for me."

"Don't you frickin' Karma me." She upped her glare. "Just because you're kind of cute doesn't mean you can get away with anything."

He pulled on her ponytail. "I'm only kind of cute?"

He was mouthwatering, but she wasn't feeling generous enough to tell him that. "Are we playing or are you going to torture me first?"

Chance brought her closer to him and whispered, with a delicate kiss below her ear. "I'll torture you after, darling. Sweet, sweet torture, and you'll beg for it."

She shivered, knowing he was right, but no way was she going to admit it. Eyes narrowed, she said, "Hardly."

"I left Ante Up at home, like you requested." Taking a pack of cards out of his pocket, he moved to the coffee table in front of the couch and sat on the floor. "You were right. It's totally inappropriate for junior to see us get it on."

She snorted derisively, but on the inside a

secret electric shock of anticipation shot up her spine.

"And to be fair to you"—he shook the cards out of their box and began to shuffle them—"I'm giving you a handicap."

"What sort of handicap?" she asked suspiciously.

He grinned devilishly. "I'm not wearing underwear."

Her gaze dropped to his pants involuntarily. She'd given herself a handicap, too—she was wearing the underwear he'd given her with the engagement ring. "Let's just get this over with."

He tipped his head and looked at her. "Then sit down, sweet pea."

She plopped inelegantly across from him and held her hands out. "I'll do the first round."

He handed her the deck and sat back.

When she shuffled the cards, a few flew out of her hands. Cursing under her breath, she added them back in and quickly dealt their cards. "Texas Hold'em, minus the betting?"

"Yes."

Nodding grimly, she dealt their two private

cards and then flipped four cards all at once. She looked at her cards. She perked up when she saw she had two pairs.

She glanced at Chance's face. He might as well have been wearing sunglasses, his gaze was so shuttered. He gazed at her steadily, waiting.

Good—his hand must suck. She gleefully gave him another card before adding the last card to the table.

She had a full house.

Exhaling happily, she tried not to wiggle as she wondered which article of clothing he was going to take off first.

"Want to go first?" he asked.

"Okay." Grinning, she turned her cards over, showing her hand. "Top that."

"Okay." He flipped his.

A straight flush.

She frowned. "How the hell did you do that?"

He shrugged. "Just luck, I guess."

Disgruntled, she sat up on her knees and defiantly took her top off, revealing the green and black bra. She smiled with satisfaction as his eyes popped. Good—let him be distracted.

"You wore the lingerie I bought you," he said, his voice deeper with desire.

"Yep." She dealt the cards.

"The panties, too?"

"Yep." She flashed him an evil grin.

"Have mercy," he murmured as he picked up his cards.

Half an hour later, they were in it. He only had on his jeans and she was down to the panties in question.

As she was about to put down the last card on the river, she looked at Chance. He hadn't looked at his cards yet. "Aren't you going to peek at them?"

"No, I'm taking this one on faith." He grinned. "The way I see it, I've been a really good boy this year. I've got a reward coming to me."

Eyes narrowed, she dropped the last card.

He flipped his cards over. "A flush," he said, sounding surprised.

"Damn it." She threw her cards in the middle and glared at him.

Leaning against the couch, Chance spread his arms. "You know the unexpected benefit of this?"

"What?"

"I get to hear you play naked." He grinned wolfishly. "It's like Christmas and my birthday all wrapped in one."

Grumbling she stood up and shimmied out of the underwear, tossing it at him. "Happy?"

He caught it in one hand and twirled it around his finger. "Almost."

She glanced at her piano. Normally, she saw it like her best friend—always there and a constant support. Right now she was having a love/hate relationship with it.

Chance wasn't going to let her off the hook for this, so she may as well rip the Band-Aid off. Taking a deep breath, she stood on nerve-wobbly legs and made her way to the bench.

The wood was cold on her butt. She'd never played naked before. When she put her hands on the keys, they were shaking. "Was stripping me down to nothing your goal, or was it just a perk?"

"It's metaphorically brilliant, isn't it?"

She wondered if he was going to stay where he was or come lord it over her, but he leaned his chin on his fist, angling toward her, across the room. She exhaled, relieved to have a little space.

Her fingers touched the keys, but they were so jittery she couldn't start. She felt the usual panic welling inside her chest, making it impossible to breathe. She closed her eyes, shaking her head, knowing she couldn't do this.

A hand rested on her head, strong and steady. She opened her eyes and met Chance's.

"KT, you could play 'Twinkle, Twinkle Little Star' and I'd love it," he said softly. "Look me in the eyes and play just for the two of us. I'm going to love whatever you pick."

"How do you know?" she managed to ask.

He cupped her face. "Because it's from you."

Staring into his eyes, she wondered if he'd really feel that way even if she played a crappy version of a children's song.

Yes, he would. Her gut knew that with unwavering faith. Holding his gaze, her fingers trembling, she began her concert in the middle, the part that she'd written with the taste of him still on her tongue.

She faltered a note, and sweat broke out on her forehead, but his expression didn't waver. He looked every bit as encouraging, as pleased, as enthralled as he did when they made love.

A hint of warmth spread through her. It was a familiar feeling—she always felt it when she played by herself. It wasn't as soothing or strong as usual, and she still felt shaky, but she also felt stronger.

Grateful.

Swallowing her fear, she suddenly wanted him to hear it—to know how she felt about him. Holding his gaze, she played for someone other than herself for the first time ever.

Then she got to the last note and stopped abruptly. She had to try a few times before she could say, "I haven't finished the rest of the song."

He gaped at her. "You wrote that?"

She shrugged, dropping her gaze. It'd sucked—she knew it.

"Karma Taylor." He leaned down until his eyes were the only thing that filled her field of vision. "You can change the world with your music. That is your purpose."

"You're being dramatic," she murmured, trying to avert her gaze.

He wouldn't let her. "People need to hear that beautiful music from your heart. Put it out yourself. Your music, your terms. You'll be happy, and you'll make a difference. It's what you're meant to do."

Right. She shrugged. He didn't know what it took to produce music. It wasn't what she did.

Hauling her up, he set her on the keys, her ass making the piano protest in a jarring cacophony. He gripped her thighs, standing between them, and leaned into her. "Thank you."

She felt him hard between her legs, and the residual fear began to melt away. "For?"

"That was a gift." He ran his hands up the side of her legs to hold her waist. "I know you were paying a bet, but you played from your heart."

Because she'd given him her heart, she realized with jarring clarity. But before she could process that any further, he kissed her with unrestrained passion.

"On the piano?" she asked when he leaned back to undo his jeans.

"Can you think of a more fitting place?"

She really couldn't. She watched as he slipped

a condom on and returned to her. Taking him in her arms, she held him close, pouring into her actions the same things she'd poured into her concerto.

He pulled her head back by her hair and kissed his way up her neck. "While you played, I felt like I was inside you," he whispered in between kisses. "It was the same feeling I get every time we make love. Hot. Exciting. Soaring."

Wanting him badly, she worked her hand between them, guiding him in.

They both moaned.

He pulled her forward, burying his head in the crook of her neck. He said nothing, but she felt like she knew everything he was thinking.

She wanted to sing the reciprocal thoughts to him.

She'd never had the urge before, but she wanted to sing her love to him. She wrapped her legs around him and clenched him in her arms, holding him close to her heart.

He plunged into her, holding her just as closely.

She wanted him to be there forever. She gasped with the feel of him moving in her, all the

while wishing he was really hers. That their engagement was real. That she was his.

Only she couldn't voice any of it.

But the piano sang her passion. It cried out with each thrust, reaching for its crescendo, sometimes happy, sometimes mournful.

"KT," Chance groaned, gripping her hips tight.

It was a plea, and she unraveled the moment she heard it. She clasped him as he came, too, holding him close, where she wanted him to be forever.

Chapter Nineteen

BIJOU CHECKED HER watch as she walked down Geary Street toward Britex Fabrics. Two minutes late. Rosalind would probably already be waiting for her.

Sure enough, Rosalind stood outside the store, her head bent over a notepad that she was scribbling on. Doodling, knowing her. She'd sketched fashion in her every spare moment from the time she'd been fourteen. The same way Bijou had scribbled down music.

She touched her purse where her small notebook was hidden away. After sitting on the pier with Will, she'd written down the snippet of words she'd heard in her head, which had magically become a refrain. She was late meeting Rosalind because on the way over, she'd had to pull over to jot down the melody that chased the lyrics — an echo of KT's concerto.

She clutched her bag, afraid to hope that it

was anything more than a fluke. After all, it'd been over a year since she'd written anything. She was hesitant to put much hope that it was the end of her drought, but it was a start.

A good start.

Rosalind looked up with a smile as she approached. "You're almost on time."

Bijou opened her mouth, intending to apologize, but she heard herself say, "I had an idea."

Her best friend froze, her mouth gaping. "For a song?"

Swallowing thickly, she nodded.

"Oh, darling"—Rosalind caught her in a hug—"that's wonderful. And about time."

Bijou laughed shakily. "I love that you get it."

"Of course I do, love. I'm an artist, too. I'm almost tempted to abandon this mission and go to Eno for a celebratory glass."

"I noticed that you said almost." Nothing deterred Rosalind when she was on a quest for the right material. Bijou opened the door to Britex Fabrics. "Speaking of celebrating, KT's getting married."

"To a man?" her best friend asked as they entered the store.

"Yes."

"Are you sure?"

Bijou shrugged. "If you'd have asked me that a couple weeks ago, I'd have said no, but then seeing them together I'm pretty sure they are."

Rosalind shook her head. "It boggles, quite frankly."

"Tell me about it." She brushed her hand along a bolt of fabric. "I don't know how to feel about it."

Rosalind headed to the back of the store, waving to the ladies manning the counter. "Do you like him? He's not a user, is he?"

Bijou knew all about users. "Chance is nothing like Brice. He looks at her with his heart in his eyes."

Rosalind stopped suddenly and whirled around. "Chance? And Karma?"

They burst out laughing, and Bijou felt the euphoria she'd felt since hanging out at the Ferry Building with Will bubble up again. Wiping her eyes, Bijou said, "I told KT if her first child was a girl, she should name her Destiny."

"I wouldn't have expected Karma to get married before you. Just goes to show that life is unexpected." Rosalind went directly to a bolt of fabric and pulled it out to inspect it. She ducked her head, but there was something tight in her expression that was about more than finding the right fabric.

"What's wrong?" Bijou asked.

"I heard from my father today." She shoved the roll back in the wall and extracted another. "You know that never goes well."

Rosalind and her father had a falling out years before, which was why Rosalind came to the states to pursue her design career. Rosalind's relationship with him had never been good. Her stories of her father always made Bijou appreciate her own dad that much more. She often felt guilty for her relationship with Anson in her friend's presence. "What did he want?"

A humorless smile twisted her lips. "What do you think? To control me."

She touched Rosalind's hand and made the offer she'd made countless times over the years. "Want to share my dad?"

"You're sweet under your rock star exterior."

She decided against the fabric in her hands and moved on. "Do you think KT will let me design her wedding dress? It'd look fantastic in my portfolio to have done Anson and Lara's daughter's dress."

"You know KT. As long as she doesn't have to be involved."

"How about you?" Rosalind looked at her with a clear gaze. "Are you ready to make your splash?"

"Yes," she said with less confidence than she'd have liked.

"Liar." She smiled and hugged Bijou with one arm. "You're going to be great. This is the moment you've been waiting for. You were born to do this."

"That doesn't mean I'm not scared."

"That's what vodka is for, love." With an excited gasp, she yanked a shimmery bolt out of the wall. "This one."

The material was red and glittery, catching the light and winking flirtatiously back. Bijou touched it, surprised by its supple softness. "Someone wants a red wedding dress?"

"Don't be daft. This is for you."

"For me?" She blinked at the material.

"For your performance next week." She pulled it out the rest of the way and tucked it under her arm. "I know I'm cutting it close, but it took me longer than usual to come up with a design. I wanted it to be perfect."

Tears clouded her eyes, and she blinked to clear them. "You don't have time to make me a dress."

Rosalind looked at her like she said she liked to eat babies. "I always have time for you, Bijou. Especially when you need me."

"And that's now?" she asked uncertainly.

"Yes, of course. You look like you're holding it together, but you're a mess on the inside. But you have nothing to worry about. You wrote music today."

"Just the refrain," she pointed out.

"That's how it starts, love. First one line, then another. And this dress I'm making for you"—she pointed at the fabric—"is your armor. You can't fail. The world will see you as you're meant to be seen, and you'll have everything you've ever wanted."

That was why she loved Rosalind. She grabbed her friend and squeezed her tight. "I love you."

"I love you, too, but don't strangle me."

Laughing and wiping under her eyes, she let go. Rosalind went to the counter and asked for a length of fabric, chatting amicably with the shop lady as the woman cut the swath of fabric.

Rosalind wouldn't even let Bijou pay for the fabric, saying it was her part in helping her succeed the same way Bijou had helped her when she first started her business. Outside, Rosalind turned to her. "Is it time for that glass of wine? Or a cappuccino? The Nespresso café is just down the way. "

Bijou looked at her watch. "I have to go. I need to work out and then I have to get ready. For a date, before you begin interrogating me."

Rosalind frowned. "With whom?"

"A guy. Just a guy," she clarified.

"You're holding out on me." Her friend frowned. "This isn't normal. What's wrong with him?"

He was a musician but no way in hell was she telling Rosalind that. "Nothing. I told you, he's just a guy."

"I don't believe you." Rosalind leaned in. "You like him, don't you? Is he the reason you were inspired?"

"Would I glom on to another man like that again, after what happened with Brice?" She kissed her friend's cheeks. "Thank you! I'll call you."

"Wait—"

She waved over her shoulder as she dashed off for the Sutter/Stockton garage, where she'd parked her car. Her date really wasn't for hours, but she needed time to prep. A long bath was in order—and a long talk with herself on why going out with Will Shaw was such a bad idea.

**When Will texted to arrange to pick her up, she told him she'd meet him at the club where his friend was playing. It seemed cooler, plus it gave her time to settle her nerves. They were full-blown tonight, like the first time she'd ever performed, when she was six. Not even her extended workout had helped calm her.

She arrived at 50 Mason Social Club and showed the doorman her ID. He gave it a cursory glance and waved her in.

It was dimly lit inside, the bar was on the left and the stage at the far end to the right. It was still early, so people weren't in full swing yet. Most were gathered around the bar, drinking and talking.

Bijou saw Will up front by the stage talking to the musicians who were setting things up. As if he sensed her, he turned around and smiled.

The butterflies in her belly took flight with a vengeance. Taking a deep breath, she slowly walked over to him.

He watched her approach, his thoughts undecipherable.

She kept his gaze, hoping her thoughts were just as inscrutable. She didn't want him to see how out of whack she felt, meeting him. She hadn't gone on a date since —

Well, since the first time she'd gone out with Brice, and even that hadn't been a proper date. He hadn't asked her — it'd been more of a hook-up. In fact, he'd just assumed she'd go back to his house with him.

She had, and she hated herself for it.

Now wasn't the time to dwell. She looked at

Will and vowed that she'd be different this time. She had value. She'd act like it.

Walking right up to him, she tipped her head and said, "Hey."

"Hey." A slight smile curved his lips as if he knew she was playing it cool and was willing to let her keep up the pretence. He took her hand and squeezed it.

Damn. She pouted knowing it was her own fault he didn't kiss her. Mental note: best not to cut off her nose to spite her face.

Before she could kiss him, Will turned her to face the guys on stage. "George, Bennett, this is Bijou. Bijou, these guys don't look it, but they're actually decent musicians."

She smiled genuinely as they guffawed.

George shook her free hand and said, "We knew this knucklehead when he was touring with Springsteen, before he went off the deep end and decided to become a shrink."

"Who does that?" she asked, only partly meaning it as a joke.

"Right?" George shrugged incredulously. "It's totally incongruous."

"Don't you guys need to finish setting up?" Will put his hand on her lower back. "You're on in ten."

George waved his hand. "Time is just an agreement, and tonight we've agreed to be loose acquaintances."

Shaking his head, Will led her to the couch closest by the stage. "Can I get you a drink?"

"A light beer is good," she said. She sat down and watched him go to the bar and order.

He came back with their beers almost instantly and sat next to her. He handed her drink over and touched it with his. "I like seeing you outside of my office, Bijou."

Yes, but she felt safer there. She took a sip of the beer and tried to center herself. "How do you know George and Bennett?"

"I've played with George, and I've known Bennett a long time, but just socially." He sipped his pint, his eyes on her. "I'm happy you joined me tonight."

"I almost didn't want to," she said honestly.

"I know." He smiled as he took her hand. "I'm not a threat, Bijou."

"Oh, you're a big threat and nothing you say will convince me otherwise."

He started to say something but the band members filed onstage and picked up their instruments. Will's attention went to the stage, wholly and eagerly. "I can't wait to have you hear their opening and tell me what you think."

She nodded politely, not expecting much. She knew she was jaded, but how could she not be? She'd grown up with the greats hanging out in her living room.

The band stood on stage, everyone ready, and then the trombone player let one long, loud note rip, and they all joined in, vibrant and enthusiastic.

Bijou sat up, alert.

"Not bad, right?" Will said in her ear.

"Pretty good actually," she replied, her head bopping to the music.

"Let's dance." Before she could so much as utter a word, he tugged her to her feet and onto the empty dance floor. Whirling her into him, he began leading her expertly to the music. Closing her eyes, she let him hold her close as she moved in sync with him to the music.

As much a musician as Brice had been, he couldn't dance. She used to endure it, hating the way he hauled her around but hopeful that he'd become more in tune to her over time. He hadn't.

Will had it from the beginning. He found the rhythm of the music and invited her to join it. Dancing in his arms was freeing—heaven. She let her head fall back and let go for the first time in a long time. Joy welled in her chest, and she laughed to let it out when she couldn't contain it any longer.

Will dipped her at the end of the song, their eyes meeting, both of them breathing hard. He lowered his head, his gaze on her lips. Their mouths brushed lightly, their breaths mingling.

He lifted her upright, holding her against him. She felt the beat of his heart against hers, and she pressed against him, wanting—

"We've got a good friend in the audience tonight," George's voice boomed, breaking their spell. "Maybe with a little encouragement he'll come up to play a song with us."

The crowd cheered for him.

But Will's eyes were on her. "I better just get this over with."

"Do it." She patted his chest and went to sit back down.

He hopped on stage and accepted the guitar he was handed.

Bijou watched him sling it over his shoulder, her heart sinking. This was where he got all elemental and forgot about her in everyone else's adulation.

He mumbled something to the band as he tuned the guitar. Then he leaned in his mic, looked at her, and said, "Bijou, come up and show these boys how it's done."

She froze from shock. He wanted her on stage with him. Smiling wide and bright, she hopped up to join them.

"What are we doing?" she asked, rubbing her hands on her jeans.

The band members looked at her with trepidation, but Will's gaze only held confidence. "Let's do 'You Shook Me All Night Long.'"

She laughed. "Okay. Kick it off, boys. I'll join in."

The band looked at each other, but George shrugged and cued the song. They began a rocking version that had her tapping her toes in time.

She felt Will's unwavering gaze on her face, and she winked at him as she launched into the song. She kept it simple but strong, letting the other band members strut their stuff at the appropriate moments. It came together so cohesively, as if they'd rehearsed it hundreds of times.

They ended as abruptly as they began. The last echoes died, and the audience was utterly still.

Just when Bijou started to wonder if she'd bombed, they burst into deafening applause. She applauded back at them before turning to give the band their due.

The band members stared at her like they were seeing her for the first time. She winked at them and then turned to Will. "One more?"

He grinned at her. "We're in your thrall."

She liked that, but he knew she would. If only she had more of her song written than just a couple lines — she'd test it out tonight.

Another time. This wasn't about her. "'Sweet Home Alabama?'"

Will and the band began, and she waited for her cue. She owned the stage as she belted out the words. She strutted, knowing she held the audience in the palm of her hand.

It felt good.

On the last note, she blew a kiss to the crowd and hopped off stage to thunderous applause. She gave the guys a thumbs up and walked back to her seat. Picking up her beer, she tried to keep her elation to herself.

The glow of performing carried through the next few songs until they began to play her song—the one Brice stole. She stiffened at the first words. Not able to bear hearing any of it, she went outside to get air.

She was standing against a lamppost, trying to calm herself when Will came out.

"They took a break," he explained at her questioning look. Taking her hand, he faced her. "What happened?"

"That was the song. The one Brice stole from me." She shrugged with nonchalance she didn't feel.

Understanding lit his expression. "Want to tell me how it went down?"

"Not really." She gave him a small smile. "We

were dating, and I wrote the song for us to perform, but he thought he could do it better on his own. It is what it is. I was too trusting, and I learned a lesson."

Will traced a line on her cheek. "You're supposed to trust those you love."

"You should have better sense about who you love though."

"You can't help who you fall in love with." He moved up against her.

She swallowed, not sure what he meant, not sure she wanted to know. So she lifted her head defiantly. "He may have stolen my song, but I'm getting my game back. The concert is going to cinch things."

"It will," he agreed. "You're too good not to stick the ending."

She tried to smile confidently but failed. She had one refrain and a vague melody to show for the last year. That was pathetic, not good. "I wish I were that sure," she said in a small voice that wasn't like her at all.

He lifted her chin and gazed into her eyes with calm certainty. "You nailed it out there tonight.

You're a pro, and you have talent, Bijou. It's normal to feel fear, but don't let it get in your way. You have a destiny, and it's on the stage. You're a rock star, deep down. You just need to claim it."

His words bolstered her in a way no one's had, not even her daddy's. She smiled at him. "You're being a therapist now."

"No." He touched her face. "I'm being a friend."

Chapter Twenty

$\mathcal{K}$T STUMBLED THROUGH her parent's house. Coffee. It was all she asked for. She knew it was late in the day but hopefully there would still be a little left in the main kitchen from morning.

She sighed in relief when she saw Bijou was the only one sitting in the kitchen. Her sister had sheet music she was staring at and a glass of something murky and green.

Then she remembered how Bijou had thrown her under the bus, and she stiffened.

Bijou looked up. "Are you just getting up?" she asked carefully.

KT shot her a glare and went to the cabinet to pull out a cup. She reached for the carafe on the counter.

Her sister sighed. "Just let me know how long you're going to harbor this grudge so I can prepare myself."

Part of her wanted to throw her arms around

Bijou, but the bigger part of her said, "How does the end of time sound?"

"Like what I'd expect." Her sister pushed her glass of gook toward her. "Have some juice. It'll perk you up better than the coffee."

"Gee, that looks appetizing." KT frowned at her. "Are you just getting up too?"

Bijou's cheeks flushed, and she ducked her head. "Don't be crazy. I always wake up earlier than you."

"Yeah, but today that's relative." KT studied her sister. "You're blushing. You never blush, not even when you were five and you came out of the bathroom with your dress tucked in your My Little Pony underwear."

"It's a hot flash."

"You're twenty-seven. You're too young for hot flashes." KT stared at her over the rim of her coffee cup. "I suspect you've been up to no good. Betray any other sisters lately?"

"Let it go. Besides"—Bijou pointed at her—"you're the one who's been up to all sorts of shenanigans."

"Shenanigans?" KT arched her brow.

"You're the one who got engaged out of the blue, to a man you barely know." Bijou returned her gaze steadily. "If that doesn't reek of shenanigans I don't know what does."

"You sound upset."

Her sister shrugged. "Because I'm your best friend and you didn't even hint that things were that serious between you and Chance? Why would I be upset?"

Before she could say anything, her mother breezed in with an armful of packets and brochures. "There you are, Karma. I was just about to try the cottage."

She and her sister exchanged a look. Bijou was the one who said, "What's all that, Mom?"

"Thoughts." Lara smiled wide as she set it all on the breakfast table. "Lots of wonderful thoughts for the wedding."

KT's stomach clenched. "You should be focusing on the concert, Mom. The wedding isn't a big deal."

"Of course it's a big deal." Her mother looked at her like she'd lost her mind. "It's not every day my firstborn gets married."

"You never know with KT," Bijou said.

She stuck her tongue out at her sister.

Bijou crossed her eyes back at her.

"Girls, do I need to remind you you're adults now?" Lara shook her head as she spread out the brochures.

Bijou leaned over to look. "I get to pick my own maid of honor dress. KT's likely to pick camouflage."

"Who said you're my maid of honor?"

"Scott's on his honeymoon, so I'm your only choice. Besides, I look better in ruffles."

KT turned to her mom. "No ruffles."

"Of course not, sweeting." Lara flipped the pages of bridal dress book. "I was thinking lace. A lovely cascade of lace."

"Lace?" KT shuddered.

"At the risk of muddying the waters," Bijou started, "Rosalind said she'd make KT's dress."

Their mom closed the book, her face beaming. "That's perfect. Rosalind is so talented. Do you think she can see us today?"

Today? KT felt panic well in her throat, cutting off her air. This was going too far.

"Is that your ring?" Her mother gasped as she reached for KT's hand and held it up to inspect it closer. "This is absolutely perfect, sweeting. He knows you so well."

"He does, doesn't he?" The irony wasn't lost on her.

"It's very nice," Bijou said softly. She looked up, sadness and regret in expression. "I'm happy for you, KT."

She took her hand back, wanting to tell them not to get too attached to the ring because it was going back in a couple weeks.

"I made some calls, Karma." Her mom pulled some scribbled notes. "Elton can't make it to officiate the ceremony on such short notice, but he sends his love. But don't worry, I've contacted Conan."

"I need to go." She pushed away from the table. On her way out of the kitchen, she said, "I have a piano lesson with my student. See you guys later."

"Karma —"

But she was already down the hall, walking faster and faster until she was running out of the house.

The piano lesson with Ashley was a lie, but because she'd said she was going there, she figured she should—at least for a little while. Outside she hopped in a cab and asked him to drop her off at the foundation.

Gwen wasn't anywhere to be found, but Lola was sitting at a table with a teenager. They were both tapping away at laptops. Lola bobbed her head up and down to whatever music was piping in through her earphones. The girl looked completely engrossed, biting the corner of her lip in concentration.

Lola looked like a Barbie come to life. KT and Bijou had always shared an aversion to Barbie, so she'd been prepared not to like the woman, but beyond the blond facade, Lola was a funny, interesting person.

KT had intended to walk by and leave them undisturbed but then Lola looked up, smiled, and took her earbuds out. "KT! Is it your day to tutor?"

"Not really. I just thought I'd stop by to check things out." She looked around. "Gwen isn't here today?"

"She's at her shop this afternoon. She got an idea for a series. You know she's a gourd artist, right?"

KT leaned forward. "To tell you the truth, I have no idea what that means."

"You wouldn't be the first one. Stop by her shop sometime. Gwen's an amazing artist. Seeing is believing." She pointed to her laptop. "I've got to get back to work. Deadline, you know. Carly and I have a writing date."

The teenager glanced up and smiled briefly before returning to her work.

Lola jerked her thumb toward the music room. "Ashley's in there. I'd go check her out, if I were you."

KT rolled her eyes. "In case I haven't gotten my fill of agro-pounding music lately?"

"Because I think you'll be surprised." Lola raised her eyebrows.

Frowning, not sure what to think, KT got up and strode toward the room.

It wasn't empty the way she'd expected. Ashley—Spike—was in there playing.

Playing really well.

KT stood in the doorway, gaping, her jaw on the floor. Ashley played with command, like the piano was her slave and beloved all at once, just the way it should be. She didn't recognize the song, which made her think the girl wrote it.

Lola was right. She was blown away.

The keys crashed, and Ashley whirled around with a glare. "Are you spying on me?"

KT smiled at the irony. Stepping into the room, she nodded at the piano. "You lied to me."

The girl just looked more belligerent. "No, I didn't. You just didn't listen to what I was saying."

"Touché." She pulled up a chair. "When did you write that?"

"How do you know I wrote it?"

"Because I know music, and I've never heard that before." Stretching, she trailed her fingers over the keys, picking out part of the dark melody. "It was good."

The girl looked at her suspiciously. "It was?"

"No, I lied. It was frickin' fantastic." She gave the girl a flat look. "I don't say that lightly."

"No kidding." Some of her bravado fell away, and she played with the zipper on her pleather jacket. "You really think it was okay?"

"Better than okay. Just maybe consider this one part"—she nudged the girl over and sat on the bench to play the section—"like this."

Ashley listened to her play the section over in the different key. "It's more sinister that way."

"Definitely more layered. It's just a thought. There's no right answer. It's your composition, so you need to do what you think is right." She sat back and stared at her. "I don't get it. Where'd you learn to play like that?"

Ashley shrugged. "I just picked it up. There was a crappy piano in the school auditorium."

"Then why'd you let me bug you about scales and stuff if you already know how to play?"

"I don't know." The girl shrugged, looking down. "It was just kind of nice to have someone care."

Guilt stabbed KT in the chest. She could be accused of not caring either—she'd just been trying to get out of the concert.

But she did care, she realized.

"Whoa." Ashley pointed to her hand. "That's some rock."

She grinned, remembering her own reaction. "Right?"

"Are you getting married?"

"Kind of." She sighed.

"You don't sound happy about it." Then the girl frowned. "You'll still come here even though, right?"

She hadn't thought about it. She'd thought she'd keep this gig until the concert and then leave. But now, Ashley needed her. That sort of talent needed to be nurtured. It wasn't easy doing it on your own. But she wasn't the most nurturing person. As a teacher, she sucked. But maybe she could find someone who'd take Ashley under her wing. "I'm not going anywhere."

The teenager smiled for the first time—a true smile that lit her eyes.

Her fingers itched to pull Ashley into a hug. But she knew better, so she nudged the kid with her shoulder. "Play me more, Spike."

"Okay," the teenager said, showing enthusiasm for the first time.

KT closed her eyes and listened, amazed that talent like this could have been hidden for so long without anyone noticing.

Like yours? a little voice that sounded suspiciously like her mom's asked.

Shut up, she told it, even though she saw the irony.

Chapter Twenty-one

AS HE GOT dressed for his meeting with Leif, Chance glanced at KT, who lay on his bed scowling at the TV as she flipped through stations. Something was bothering her, but she denied it the couple times he'd asked.

It surprised him how much he wanted her to confide in him — how much he wanted to fix whatever was bothering her.

"You should just go naked," she said without taking her eyes off the screen.

"You think that'll increase my chances of getting hired?"

"I'd definitely hire you if you showed up naked." She grinned at him as she turned the TV off.

He looked at her, lounging in his bed wrapped in just the sheets, and his chest filled with emotion. He wanted this — forever. He didn't think of himself as a domestic guy, but he could see this as his future, with KT, and it was strangely appealing.

She waved her hand to him after he'd put his shoes on and slipped his wallet into his pocket. "Come here."

He went to her.

Grabbing the front of his shirt, she pulled him down to her and gave him a bone-melting kiss. "Kick ass," she said against his lips.

Nodding, he touched her cheek. "Thank you."

She turned over and reached for one of the cookies she'd stashed on the bedside table. "Let the pig back in before you leave."

He went to the bathroom and opened the door. Ante Up ran out, annoyed, and headed straight to KT like it wasn't her who suggested locking him in there in the first place. She didn't want him to see "mommy and daddy getting it on."

"Don't feed him cookies," Chance said, strapping his watch to his wrist. "He's getting chubby."

"Don't listen to him, Ante Up," she said to the pig. "You're just healthy."

The porker snorted, as if he didn't believe it either.

Chance drove to his lunch meeting with Roger Leif with a smile on his face. It was still firmly in place as he walked through the restaurant to the booth where Leif sat.

The man slouched in the corner, toying with the napkin under his drink. When he looked up, Chance knew immediately that something wasn't right.

He sat down and faced it. "You look like you don't have good news, Roger."

Leif scowled at him. "I hear you're getting married."

"I'm not sure what that has to do with the job."

"I need someone hungry, with an edge. I can't hire you if you're happy." Leif made a face as if happiness tasted bitter to him.

"You think my getting married will affect the way I work?" he asked incredulously.

"Of course it will. It's the end of a winning streak," the man said glumly.

"Actually, I see it as the beginning of a bigger streak," Chance said, looking the man in the eye. He sat back, thinking. "Where did you hear about my engagement?"

Roger shrugged. "What does it matter?"

He knew the answer, though: Tiffany Woods.

He supposed he knew exactly what she'd told her boss.

As if reading his thoughts, Leif said, "You've put me in a bad place, Chance. I have no choice. Tiffany brought me more qualified candidates."

"Everyone has a choice, Roger, and you thought I was more than qualified when we met." Normally, he'd have countered Leif's arguments and brought him around to his way of thinking, but Chance didn't have the stomach for it. Maybe Leif was right—maybe meeting KT had changed his drive. Or maybe his priorities were skewed in the right direction.

In any case, he had no desire to justify himself or his relationship, and he certainly wasn't giving up KT. So he stood and held out his hand. "It would have been good, Roger. Thanks for the opportunity."

"That's it?" The man stared sourly at Chance's hand. "You're not going to try to dissuade me?"

"Why would I want to?" Chance lowered his hand and looked the man in the eye. "You've shown me that you trust the wrong information. That's the kiss of death for a gambler. Why would I align myself with that? I have skills, especially in speculating. If you don't want to use them, I'll find someone else who does."

He stood up with a nod and began to leave.

"Chance, buddy"—the chair screeched as Leif stood—"maybe I was a little hasty."

He turned and looked over his shoulder. "You were definitely hasty, but that's your loss."

"Maybe we can come to some sort of agreement."

Chance smiled. "I find that unlikely, but thank you for the effort."

He walked out of the restaurant, not feeling the least bit remorseful.

KT was still in his bed when he returned, snuggled with Ante Up. They were both engrossed in a movie, but she frowned at him when he entered. "What are you doing back already?"

"Joining you two." He tossed his wallet on the dresser, kicked off his shoes, and climbed on the bed next to her.

"What happened?" She turned to face him, her hand on his cheek as she searched his face. She blinked incredulously. "You didn't get the job? How is that possible?"

"Tiffany sabotaged my application. I guess she wasn't pleased that I didn't go for her."

"He didn't give you a job because of her?" KT frowned. "Isn't he the boss?"

"Yeah, but apparently she has him by the balls, and I really don't care." He nuzzled her neck. "Are there any cookies left? I have a craving for something sweet."

KT lifted his head, her hands on either side of his face. "You can't just throw everything away on an engagement that isn't real."

"Not real, KT?" He sobered. "I'm not sure how much more real anything can be."

"Don't buy into the delusion."

"This is reality, sweet pea." He kissed her, showing her with his lips just how real they were.

"This is sex," she said in between the kisses, "not reality. Reality is getting the job you wanted."

Rolling on top of her, he pressed his hard-on against her hip. "My priorities have changed. That job isn't what I want most now."

"Oh, hell no." She yanked herself away from him and kicked her legs to get free of the tangled sheets. "Don't go there."

"Too late." He sat up, knowing what she was feeling because he felt it, too. But there was one difference between the two of them. "Don't run away from what you feel for me, Karma. Don't run from me."

"This is just lust."

"Yes, but it's also love."

"Bullshit," she yelled, falling off the bed in her struggles.

"Play me. One round of strip poker," he said. "If you win, I go back to Leif and accept his terms."

She pulled at her hair, like she was going crazy. "This isn't a game."

"You're right. It's not a game." He took her hands and pulled her into him. To him, it was forever. If only he could get her to see that, too.

Chapter Twenty-two

BEING ENGAGED WASN'T all it was cracked up to be. If she'd known she'd be required to attend parties, she might have thought of a different way of diverting her mom. KT yanked on a pair of pants, annoyed that she had to get dressed for the impromptu engagement party Lara was hosting tonight.

Except her mom was all excited about the "sacred union," as she called it, and it was kind of sweet. KT played along because she couldn't bring herself to squash her mother's enthusiasm.

The one upside was since they'd announced their engagement, no one had talked about her performing in the concert. So there was that.

She grabbed the shirt off the bed and pulled it over her head. It got tangled in her hair, which her mother had told her to leave down, and then got caught on the ring Chance had given her. She tugged hard, not caring about the sound of fabric ripping.

Damn it, she wasn't even really engaged.

She stared at the ring. She'd never tell anyone, but she loved it. It made her sad thinking about the day she'd have to give it back.

A lot of things made her sad about breaking up with Chance, which was crazy because their relationship was a sham. Even though every kiss, every touch, every conversation felt real.

She really wanted it to be real.

But not at the expense of his happiness. He was so gung-ho about what he saw as his purpose. Just because she didn't have one didn't mean he shouldn't. She didn't want him to look back in the future and regret being with her because it'd cost him a good opportunity.

Pouting, she put on her shoes and went to the main house. She needed a drink—and to corner Chance to make sure he'd made things right with Roger Leif.

Chance was already there, standing with a tumbler in his hand, and Ante Up investigating close by. He was talking to Bijou and another man who had his hand on her sister's back.

KT frowned and marched over to them. "Who

are you?" she asked the dude straightaway.

Bijou rolled her eyes. "Will, this is KT. Aren't you glad she missed all her sessions now?"

Will smiled and shook her hand. "Hello, KT. For the record, I don't believe you're as crazy as Bijou says you are."

Bijou hit his shoulder, laughing.

Holy crap. KT gaped at them. Her sister was in love with a therapist, only he looked just her type.

"No kiss for me, sweet pea?" Chance slid his arm around her waist and kissed her lightly. "We missed you. Were you primping again?"

"Yeah, right." She turned to study the therapist. Her mom would have said he had a nice aura, and she'd have been right. More than that, he looked at Bijou like the sun rose and set on her.

She wished Chance looked at her that way. She turned her frown on him. How did he look at her?

He bent to kiss her neck, whispering, "If you don't stop looking at me that way, I'm going to sling you over my shoulder despite all the cookies you ate last night."

"Karma, sweeting, there you are." Her mother swept toward them. Tonight she was in full diva-mother-of-the-bride mode, wearing a pale blue sequined top and a matching silk sarong skirt, with silver stilettos. She had a million silver bracelets on her wrists and one dangling feather earring, her hair in an elaborate braid at the back of her head. Her eyes were smoky and her lips were sultry—and frowning. "What in the name of Buddha are you wearing, Karma?"

KT looked down at herself. "Clothes."

"Really, sweeting, you look like you're on your way to a funeral, not your own wedding." She looked accusingly at Bijou.

Her sister threw her hands out defensively. "I'm not her keeper. She doesn't even like me much right now."

"Don't be silly, Bijou. She loves you."

Chance wisely interrupted at that moment. "Lara, you look stunning. It's good that I met KT first."

Her mother laughed delightedly, giving him a kiss on his cheek. "We'll keep you, darling, and I'm so happy you're ours now."

282

KT felt him tense, and she immediately turned to make sure everything was okay. Outwardly, he looked the same, but she knew that was his poker face in place. The hand at her waist gripped harder.

She remembered how he wanted to set roots, and that his family had been taken from him in one fell swoop. Her heart broke for him all over again. It must have meant so much to have a family again. She covered his hand with hers and kept him to her.

Except it wasn't in the cards. She was going to take it away when they broke up, just like she'd cost him the job he really wanted.

The doorbell rang, and Nellie yelled from the hallway. "I'll get it."

"Where's Dad?" Bijou asked, craning her head as though he could be hiding somewhere in the empty room.

"I distracted him while he was changing." Their mother flashed a sultry smile. "He'll be down shortly."

KT turned to Chance and mouthed, Save me.

He chuckled and kissed her temple.

Nellie escorted her friend Griffin and his

woman, Nicole, into the living room. Grif looked like the rock star that he was in cowboy boots and a flashy shirt and a big white smile. Nicole looked like she belonged right alongside him, in red knee-high boots and a sassy dress.

Grif winked at KT but went to Lara first, giving her a big hug.

Lara closed her eyes and squeezed him back, and then held him at arm's length, looking at him fondly. "You did good, Griffin. Your new record is holding at number one, and that's not even your greatest accomplishment."

He looked at Nicole with love in his eyes.

The KT of several weeks ago would have pretended to gag, but this engaged, foreign KT got misty eyed.

Grif greeted Bijou and then turned to KT. "Karma Taylor."

She flipped him off.

Laughing, he grabbed her in a hug. "There's the KT I know and love. You scared me when I found out you were engaged. I thought the world was ending." He turned to Chance. "Griffin Chase. KT and I go way back."

"Chance Nolan."

"You're getting a diamond here," Grif said. "A rough one, but flawless nonetheless."

She elbowed him. "Shut up."

Grif swung his arm around her shoulder and motioned Nicole to meet Chance. The four of them chatted while other people arrived. Bijou and her man joined them, launching into an animated discussion of a friend they discovered they all had in common.

Fine with KT. It gave her a moment to lean into Chance and ask, "Have you talked to Roger yet?"

He shook his head, sipping his drink.

"You should call him."

"This probably isn't the best time to discuss this," he said for her ears only.

"It's been on my mind a lot." She gripped his arm. "I don't want you to miss this chance."

"I'm not sure it's such a great opportunity."

"Since when?"

"Since it'd mean working with a person who'd hire someone like Tiffany Woods." He looked at her. "What brought this on?"

She shrugged, worrying the hem of her shirt. He felt this way now, but one day he'd wonder what if, and he'd see her as the reason he didn't have what he wanted. "I guess in a couple weeks all this will be over," she said to reassure herself, "then you can go for it."

He faced her, his face a stony mask. "What if I don't want it to be over?"

"It has to be over," she said, feeling miserable.

"Karma," one of her mom's friends called out. "Are you going to play for us tonight?"

There was a wave of laughter through the room.

KT stiffened. Was that mockery in the woman's voice?

Chance squeezed her hand. "It's okay," he whispered to her. "Don't pay attention."

How could she not? Everyone was watching her. They all knew—a fair number of them had been there that day when she'd freaked out at the piano.

Bile burned at the base of her throat, and she swallowed it down, painful and bitter.

It was always going to feel this way, too.

She pulled her hand from Chance's. "How can

you be with me? I'm broken, and I'm just bringing you down, too."

"KT—"

Shaking her head, she hurried out of the room. She needed air. She needed to get away.

Her dad was coming down the hall, his blissed-out and happy expression morphing into confusion as she rushed past. "Karma, where are going?"

She made a beeline for the door. If she could just get to the hedge and hop over—

Chance's hands closed on her shoulders, and he swung her around.

She shook her head. "I can't do this."

"Breathe, babe." He stroked her hair. "It's all going to be okay."

"It's not." She tugged at the ring. Damn it—it wouldn't come off.

Her mother joined them, concern softening her gaze. "Sweeting, what are you doing?"

KT struggled with the ring. "I can't do this."

Bijou stood behind their mom. "KT—"

"Damn it." She tried to pry the ring off. "Damn it. It won't come off."

Chance took her hands in his and forced her to look at him. "Tell me what's going on."

She looked into his eyes and felt her heart break. "I'm calling it all off."

"Why?" he asked calmly.

"Because it's all wrong." It killed her, but she stepped back. "You're losing what you wanted most because of this fake engagement."

Her mother gasped. "Fake?"

Bijou groaned.

"I'm coming clean," she said to Chance. Then she turned to her mom. "Chance and I were faking seeing each other to get me out of having to perform. I thought if you were distracted by the other things I was doing, you'd let me out of the concert and still let Bijou perform."

"Oh, Karma." Her mother shook her head.

"I'm sorry I lied to you." She yanked at the ring, which still wouldn't come off.

"It hasn't been a lie," Chance said.

They all turned to him.

Chance was only looking at her though. He pulled her closer, hands at her waist. "Our feelings haven't been a lie," he said softly, just for her.

She'd never feel his hands again after this, and that made her feel wretched. "You wouldn't have proposed to me if it weren't for my mom and the cannibal."

"I disagree."

"You're just being stubborn."

"I'm telling you how I feel. My feelings haven't been a lie. Even our first kiss wasn't a lie. We may have justified getting together for other reasons, but our relationship was always true. You're being a coward."

Her eyes narrowed. "I'm trying to be nice here, to give you space to make the career move you wanted to make, and you're calling me names."

"I don't want you to be nice. I want you to be yourself," he said. "You're running away because you're scared. You were scared to play the piano, and you're scared to admit how you really feel about me."

She stepped out of his arms. "You don't know everything about me, Chance."

"No, I don't, but I know quite a bit. I know you love your sister so much you'd do anything for her, including come up with crazy, complicated schemes. I know you make music that's from the divine. I know you love teaching piano to a surly teenager." His voice dropped low, just for her. "I know the look you get when I slide my hand in your pants, and how you sound just before you come. I know you sleep with your hands tucked under your cheek, like a princess. I know you laugh from your belly and how selective you are about the people you let hear you laugh. I know that you have a lot of strength and determination on the inside, and that you can be stubborn as hell. You can do anything you want, even play in front of people, if you decide to let yourself do it."

She would not tear up. "It's not that easy."

Chance crossed his arms. "Actually, it is."

The ring suddenly popped off her finger, like it hadn't been stuck at all. She stared at it, not wanting to give it up. But she wasn't who he thought she was, so she held it out to him.

At first, she didn't think he was going to take it, but then he slipped it in his pocket. "For the record, I never pretended, KT."

Her eyes stung with tears. She watched him

leave out the front door, the click of the handle very final.

Turning, she looked helplessly at her mom, dad, and sister. Bijou sighed, and her dad looked like he wanted to cry for her, too. But it was the pity in her mom's eyes that got to her. She turned and ran, not unaware that she was really good at that.

Chapter Twenty-three

$\mathcal{W}$ILL CAME TO her immediately after she re-entered the parlor. "Is everything okay?"

Bijou shook her head. "No, it's not."

Taking her hand, he started to guide her back into the hall, but she stopped him. Her parents were out there, and she didn't want to see them right at this moment. "This way," she said, leading him through the crowded room and out the terrace doors to the courtyard.

They walked in silence to the gazebo. She let go of his hand when they got there and began to pace. "KT broke off the engagement."

"Is she okay?"

"I don't think so. She loves him. It's so blazingly clear." She winced, thinking of the shattered look in her sister's eyes. Normally, Bijou would have followed her, but KT still wasn't really talking to her.

It made her feel powerless.

And the feeling of that she lacked power only worsened when she thought of the concert. "Mom's going to mandate that KT perform again. But she won't, which means I'm out of luck, too."

When Will didn't say anything, she stopped and faced him. "Well? You've got nothing to say?"

He sat on a stone slab, looking comfortable. Unflappable. Then he asked, "You don't need this concert, Bijou. Go out on your own terms. Do your own concert. People will want to hear you."

"You don't understand." She shook her head. "I can't."

"Why not? You don't need mommy and daddy's permission."

She crossed her arms and glared at him. "This isn't what I came to you for."

"Why did you come to me?"

"Because I was upset," she said, her voice raising in frustration.

"Who are you more upset for, Bijou? Your sister, or yourself?"

She recoiled, feeling like she'd been slapped. "What?"

"It's a valid question."

"You're doing it again." She yanked the front of his shirt, until he stood in front of her. "I don't need a therapist right now. I need a boyfriend."

"You don't act like it."

She threw her hands in the air. "I maul you every chance I get. How much more direct can I be?"

He wrapped his arms around her waist. "Bijou, do you want me to be your boyfriend?"

Faced with the question, she paused. Her heart pounded, knowing she'd only have one shot at this.

"If you want me, you're going to have to accept all parts of me," he said, facing her head on. "I'm a therapist, but I'm also a musician, and that's never going to change."

That was the part that got her each time. She pulled away from him and began to pace again. "This wasn't the discussion I wanted to get into."

"But you brought it up." Will crossed his arms and stood in her path, not letting her evade him. "If you want a boyfriend, you've got to deal with the whole package."

"What whole package?" She mirrored his

stance, scowling at him. "The one where one minute you're nice to me and the next you treat me like crap?"

"If you assume every relationship is like the one you had with one selfish ass, you're in for a lonely, miserable life." He pinned her with his gaze. "Do you even know what a real boyfriend does for his woman?"

She poked her finger in his chest. "A real boyfriend listens."

"Yes. And he boosts her up when she feels insecure. He helps her when she needs help, like with a song she's writing." He gave her a flat look. "Most of all, he protects her at all costs, even when it's from herself."

"I don't need protecting."

"You don't get to pick and choose." He held out his arms. "This is the whole package. No substitutions. Either you want it, or you don't."

She glared at him. "You're missing the point."

"No, Bijou. You are." He smiled sadly at her and backed out of the gazebo.

She took a step toward him, but he'd already turned his back, leaving her alone. A brisk wind gusted through the trees, and she wrapped her arms around herself, feeling alone—and angry, because she didn't have to be.

Chapter Twenty-four

THE PIGLET TROTTED through the staged apartment, investigating the new space. Chance followed less enthusiastically.

It was in the Marina, close to his boat slip. The top floor apartment had a small balcony where you could sit and watch the sailboats cruise on the bay. The view was amazing—with a panorama that spanned from the Golden Gate Bridge to Alcatraz. It had two bedrooms and was a pet-friendly building with an outdoor space where Ante Up would enjoy rooting around.

Best of all, the living space was large, with a huge connecting dining room that could easily fit a handmade French grand piano.

"It's kind of perfect, isn't it?" Chance said, hands in his pockets.

His porcine roommate lifted his snout in the air, agreeing.

"I know why you like it here. I saw the way

you were looking at that poodle that got into the elevator with us."

Ante Up gave him a piggy leer.

"The only problem is I'm not sure we have any reason to stay in San Francisco."

The pig looked at him like he was an idiot.

He was. Chance couldn't disagree.

The clacking of the real estate agent's shoes on the hardwood floor made him turn around. "What do you think?" she asked.

Chance shrugged. "This apartment is perfect."

"The great thing is that small pets are welcome."

"A definite plus."

"I hear a 'but' in your statement," the real estate agent said with a worried smile.

Because KT wasn't moving in with him. How perfect could any place be?

He shook his head. "I'm going to need to think about it."

"A place this great isn't going to stay available long. As you know, rentals are in high demand in the city."

"I'll keep all that it mind. Ante Up," he called.

His little pig came prancing out of the bathroom. Chance tipped his head to the door, thanked
the agent again, and trailed his pig out the door.

**At the Carrington-Wright mansion, Elise
sat in the front room, papers spread on the low
table in front of her. She was studying them from
over the rims of her reading glasses when they
walked in. "You look in need of refreshments."

Ante Up headed straight to her, standing next
to her and gazing up adoringly.

She scratched under his chin as she called
on the house phone for tea and snacks. Then she
waved Chance to a chair and said, "What have
you two been up to today?"

"We looked at apartments." He stretched his
legs out, exhaling. "It was exhausting."

Ante Up huffed in agreement.

"I take it you didn't find anything promising."

"We did," he said unenthusiastically.

She gave him a measuring look as one of the
maids brought in their snacks. Elise thanked her
with a warm smile and then picked up a cookie
and held out a broken-off piece to Ante Up. The

pig snatched it eagerly.

Chance looked at Elise with a raised brow.

"Really, darling, everyone needs a treat every so often."

"He's going to get fat."

"He's just big-boned," she said as she fed the pig another piece.

It was something KT would have said, and it made him yearn for her.

He looked at Ante Up, who gave him a smug grin back. "You think you're in hog heaven right now, but it's the treadmill for you later, buddy."

Ante snorted and patiently waited for more.

"Stop brooding and tell me what's wrong, Chance."

"Am I brooding?"

She gave him an amused look. "Are you really going to try to deny it?"

"No, I just wondered."

"This involves Karma, of course." At his surprised look, she rolled her eyes. "I recognize the signs from Prescott's recent foibles in love."

"She broke off our engagement."

She stared at him. "Chance, you know you've

become like my own son since you've been here?"

"Yes," he said warily.

"Then you won't take it the wrong way if I say I'm tempted to smack some sense into you."

He smiled ruefully. "Am I that hopeless?"

"Not hopeless, darling, just clueless. But you're a man. You can't help it."

"I think there was a compliment in there somewhere." He took a scone from the platter on the table. "I'm just not sure where."

"Chance, you need to decide what you want." She poured tea for both of them. "You came here to set down roots. What does that look like?"

"Like a room full of music and light, with KT curled on the couch with a guitar in her lap," he said without hesitation.

"Then you have your answer."

"More like a lot more questions."

"You seem to land on your feet, regardless." She leveled him a no-nonsense look. "So what do you want?"

"KT." It didn't require any thought.

Elise sat back. "Then get the girl."

"Okay." He nodded. "I have no idea how I'll

do that, but I will."

"Good. I like Karma, and then you'll have to come visit me."

"I'd visit you regardless."

She smiled at him. "You're a good boy. I'm glad you came to stay."

His phone rang. He looked at the unfamiliar number and apologized to Elise as he answered. "Chance Nolan."

"Chance, this is Steve Hall. We met at Roger Leif's party."

"Yes." He frowned. "How can I help you?"

"Roger said that he didn't ask you to join his firm."

"True," Chance said, wondering where this was going.

"His stupidity is my gain. My firm specializes in high-yield ventures, what others would call risky. We're in no way as big as Paragon, but we have a lot to offer, in compensation and freedom. I'm looking for forward-thinking, creative people, and from what I know of your background, you sound like a perfect addition to my team. I'd like to invite you to come in and take a look around.

Does Monday sound good?"

"That's great," he said, a little stunned. "Thank you."

"My assistant will send you the info. Looking forward to this, Chance."

"Me too." He got off the phone and turned to Elise.

"You work fast," she said with a lift of her brow.

"It's my luck."

"You make your own luck." She patted his arm. "Don't forget that, and don't let Karma forget that."

Chapter Twenty-five

"YOU DON'T LOOK your usual cheery self," Eve said as she slid a cappuccino across the bar. "I feel like I should offer you something stronger to go with your coffee."

Bijou smiled faintly, holding her cup in her hands. "Something stronger, like a cinnamon roll?"

"If you're asking for a cinnamon roll, I know something's wrong." Eve held up a finger and smiled at a couple who walked into her coffee-house. "Excuse me a sec."

Bijou nodded as she sipped her coffee. She didn't mind a moment of quiet. Not that things had been noisy at home. Just the opposite, actual-ly. KT had barricaded herself in her cottage, and her mom and dad were rehearsing for the con-cert. The noisiest thing lately had been her own thoughts, which were relentless.

The front door chimed open and Rosalind

walked in, sporting a long garment bag and a wide smile. She walked over and pulled out a stool with her foot. "You're going to drop to your knees and profess your undying love for me when you see this dress. Here, take it while I order tea."

Bijou took the bag, trying not to notice the glimmering red through its plastic window. She recognized the fabric, of course, and part of her wanted to tear open the bag and try on the dress her friend had made for her.

Rosalind ordered her beverage and came to sit next to her at the counter. "Did you look at it? It's going to look fabulous on you, if I say so myself."

Bijou stared at it longingly as she carefully folded and placed it on the stool next to her. "I'm not sure what the point is."

"Is your mother still being stubborn?"

"To put it mildly. I thought she'd relent if she knew KT was more interested in classical music, but she's enforcing her ultimatum, especially now that KT isn't really getting married."

"I can't believe KT had the wherewithal to fake an engagement." Rosalind wrinkled her nose. "Have you talked to her?"

"I've tried, but she's barricaded herself in her cottage and won't open the door except for the pizza delivery guy."

"Maybe you need to hijack him and hold her pizza hostage." She smiled her thanks to Eve, who set her tea in front of her.

"The crazy part of this whole thing is that KT seemed really upset about calling off the engagement. I think she's really in love with him." Bijou turned to her friend and lowered her voice. "Do you think it's my fault they broke up?"

"KT has the responsibility there, doesn't she?" Rosalind sipped her tea, ever pragmatic. "You know the real shame about this entire situation?"

"What?"

"The wedding dress I designed for her won't get to appear in Rolling Stone."

"You already designed her dress?" For some reason that made her really sad—for KT.

"It's perfect for her, too. Tiniest bit rock star in deference to your heritage, but simple at the same time to honor who she is." Rosalind smoothed a strand of hair back into her twist. "It's quite brilliantly done, if I say so myself."

"Great, now I feel worse."

"Try your new dress on," her friend suggested. "I promise it'll make you feel better."

She looked at the bag next to her. "I can already tell that dress is magic."

"But?"

"I won't be performing."

"You will." Rosalind patted her hand briskly. "You always work to get what you want. You'll find a way."

The only way she could see was if KT performed, and that wasn't going to happen, especially since she'd betrayed her sister.

She hadn't been learning nice things about herself.

Bijou faced her friend, lowering her voice. "Do you think I seek my parents' approval?"

Rosalind pursed her lips. "Everyone does. It's a biological imperative, I think."

"I've just been wondering if maybe I shouldn't just hold my own concert." Voicing Will's idea sounded as crazy now as it had the other night.

"That'd be risky," her best friend said, taking on her rational business mien. "But bold. You have a name, so you're not completely starting without anything. I know you don't like to capitalize on your parents, but you'd be daft not to. You have a pedigree, use it. You have what it takes. How clever of you to realize it."

Actually, Will was the clever one. He'd believed in her more than even she had herself.

She'd been thinking about that a lot, too.

"Are you writing again?" Rosalind asked.

She sighed, hanging her head. "I'm trying."

"What does that mean?"

"It means I'm forcing myself to sit down and bang out a mediocre song every afternoon."

"That's a start." Rosalind sipped her tea. "Not every song is going to be a hit, especially after a long slump like you've had. You'll be struck by inspiration."

She had been, only she'd pushed him away.

As if reading her mind, her friend said, "What happened to that bloke you went on a date with?"

"Nothing," she lied as she slipped off the stool. She picked up the garment bag. "I'm excited about this."

"Why don't I believe that?" Rosalind said with

an amused smile. She kissed Bijou's cheeks. "Try it on, darling. I may be tooting my own horn, but that dress will bring miracles."

"Good, because I need a couple miracles." Bijou waved to Eve as she left the café.

When she arrived home, she'd meant to hang up the garment bag and do a long workout. But the dress kept winking at her as she stripped out of her street clothes, and she couldn't help put it on.

It hugged her like a dream. It was a halter, snapping comfortably behind her neck and baring her shoulders. Long in the back, the shortness in the front showed off her legs. Every time she moved, it shimmied like it was breathing and alive.

She slipped on a pair of silver heels from her closet and looked in her three-way mirror. Rosalind had outdone herself. She pictured wearing it on stage, the way the light would reflect off of it, and how it'd make her pop, and she sighed sadly.

There was a light knock on her door, and her dad poked his head in when she gave the okay. His eyes widened when he saw her, and he adjusted his glasses. "I was going to ask if you wanted to go for a run, but you're not exactly dressed for it, are you?"

"Oh, Daddy." She went to him, tears in her eyes.

He opened his arms and soothed her. "There, there, Ruby Red," he crooned, the same way he always had when she was little and had a nightmare. It should have been ridiculous now, since she was a foot taller than him, but it was still comforting.

"Come sit with me." He led her to the window seat and sat with her. Lifting her chin, he frowned as he wiped the few tears that had escaped. "What's this about?"

"I made a mess of everything. I just wanted KT to perform so Mom would let me, but now I've messed up everything for KT."

Her dad smiled gently. "You need to give your sister a little credit for where she's landed herself. That girl is stubborn, but she'll figure it out. As for you . . ."

"Yes?" she prompted.

He tipped his head. "Have I told you about the time your mother and I played Harbor Fire?"

"Harbor Fire was the concert that set you and Mom on the map."

"Yes, and they rejected us from the lineup. We were two unknown kids who had nothing but a rusted out Chevy Vega and a couple beat up guitars." He smiled fondly in his memory. "Your mother and I had been trying to get a record deal for a couple years. Months of traveling in the car, camping out to save money, eating rice and beans because it was what we could afford."

"Hard to picture Mom camping out."

"It's the reason we live this way now. She vowed one day she'd have all the luxury she wanted. Determined woman, your mother."

The wonder and love in his voice made her think of Will. Her heart constricted.

"We knew that we'd make it. We just needed a break, one person to give us the space to prove what we could do. We thought it was Harbor Fire."

"And it was."

"Yes, but what you don't know is that we snuck on stage before the real opening band could and began to play. We called ourselves the pre-opening. Before anyone figured out what had happened and could come escort us off stage, we had the crowd." His eyes shone with the sweetness of memory. "Your mother had them at the first note. I still get goosebumps thinking of her singing that night. She sang from her soul, as though she was channelling angels."

He faced Bijou, his gaze clear and direct. "Do you understand what I'm telling you, Ruby Red? Decide what you want and don't take no for an answer."

She got goosebumps now. "You think I should crash the concert and sing regardless of what Mom said?"

"Of course not. I know better than to suggest such a thing." His eyes twinkled. "I'd never contradict your mother."

His tone said the contrary. She frowned, thinking through the details. "I wouldn't have a band. Your musicians wouldn't play with me unless Mom sanctioned it."

"I'm sure you'll figure out what you need to do. You're your mother's daughter. When I look at you, I see her at your age." He smiled sweetly.

315

"It's a lovely thing to see, the beauty love creates."

She kissed his cheek. "Thank you, Daddy."

He stood up. "Nice dress, by the way. You should wear it when you play your set." He winked at her and began to whistle as he strode out.

She hopped up and unzipped the dress. She was going to perform at the concert—she'd been set on that from the beginning, and she wasn't going to take no for an answer.

It'd be a good bouncing off point for her. From now on, she was in charge. Rosalind and Will were right. She was good, and she already had a name as a birthright—there was no getting away from that. She just had to get other people to realize how good she was.

It was time to own it.

First: wowing everyone at the concert, and to do that, there was only one man she wanted at her back. She just wasn't sure he'd want to hear from her.

Will answered on the second ring. "Bijou?"

His voice sent shivers of excitement up her spine, at the same moment lighting butterflies in her stomach. "I have a proposition for you."

There was a pause, and then he said, "What makes you think I want to hear it?"

"Because you like me." She exhaled all her nerves and went for it. "Because if we're going to have a relationship, I need to trust you enough to ask you to help me."

"I didn't realize we were having a relationship," he said warily.

"I'd like to change that." She paused and then added, "If you've already given up on me, I'm going to be crushed, but I'll know you weren't right for me and move on eventually."

"You'll be crushed?" he asked with interest.

She frowned. "Of course I'll be crushed. I told you numerous times that I liked you."

"Yes, but you didn't want me to be your boyfriend."

"Clearly I had no idea what I was saying. But I'm asking you to be my boyfriend now."

"Why?" he asked baldly.

"Because I miss you. Because I like talking to you, even when you reply like a shrink."

"I am a shrink."

"I won't hold that against you." She sighed.

"Secretly, I like that you're a musician, too. I like that you understand me, and that you can play with me."

"We play well together."

"We do," she said softly, thinking of the way he kissed her. "I want to play more."

"Are you sure?" he asked, just as softly.

"Yes."

"Okay."

She frowned. "Okay, what?"

"I'll be your boyfriend." She could hear the smile in his voice. "Now that that's taken care of, what do you need my help with?"

Something that felt an awful lot like love swelled in her chest. She swallowed it down—when she told him how she felt, she didn't want there to be any doubt that she meant it purely for who he was.

But for now . . . "Will Shaw, you rock."

He laughed. "So do you, Bijou Taylor, and I can't wait until the world knows it, too."

Chapter Twenty-six

HEAD DOWN, KT walked through the foundation to the music room in the back.

Ashley was already there, fingers warming up on the keyboard. She was shrouded in all black, and her hair fell forward into her face with the intensity of her playing.

KT paused to listen. Amazing—it played like a loving conversation, with whispers and moments of passion. It was something Ashley had made up on her own—maybe the girl was making it up on the fly. How did someone that young understand emotion that deep? It'd taken KT thirty years to get it.

The girl had crazy potential. It made KT feel bad about what she was about to do.

She pushed forward. "What is that noise you're making?" she called out.

Ashley lifted one hand in a brief one-finger salute and then continued playing.

KT couldn't help smiling. She was going to

miss this kid. She grabbed a chair and set it next to the bench, waiting for her to finish.

The girl went on for five more minutes before the music ran out. She stopped and faced KT with a scowl. "You better not tell me to play it in another key."

It'd been perfect the way it was—not that KT would admit that. "I'm done torturing you, Spike."

Ashley frowned, looking fierce with all her black eye makeup. "What?"

"I'm done. I'm out. You can find a teacher you like to learn from." She swallowed her sadness. Somewhere along the way, this surly girl had crawled under her skin. Just like Chance.

The bench legs screeched as Ashley pushed back from the piano. "You're just going to quit?"

"You didn't want me here to begin with," she pointed out. "You've argued with me every step of the way."

"Well, yeah." Ashley's expression said duh. "It's what teenagers do. But adults are supposed to fight back and put us in our place."

KT threw her hands in the air. "Well, excuse me if I didn't get the memo."

"You said you weren't going anywhere."

"Well, things change, kid."

Ashley's eyes narrowed, and she put her hands in her hips. "So what do you want?"

Completely lost, KT shook her head. "What do you mean?"

"What do you want to stay?" The girl waved her hand, motioning to bring it on. "You want me to practice more? You want me to study the scales? What?"

"There's no bargaining here. This is my last day."

Ashley slammed the keyboard cover down and yelled, "Well, screw you if you're giving up on me."

KT gaped at the girl and then stood up, her hand outstretched. "I'm not giving up on you."

"Yeah right." The girl barked an ugly laugh as she stomped out of the room.

"I'm not," KT called after her. Because really she was giving up on herself.

Chance's words popped into her brain for the millionth time: You're a coward.

KT wanted to deny it—they raised her hackles

each time she replayed them in her head. But she couldn't argue with him. He was right — she was totally a coward. What she was doing to Ashley was all because she couldn't man up.

It pissed her off.

"You okay in here?" Gwen asked, peeking in from the doorway.

"No."

Gwen smiled and walked in. "Ashley seemed really upset."

KT nodded. "I told her I wasn't going to give her more lessons."

"Bummer." Gwen sat on the bench and ran her fingers across the keys in a jaunty rendition of a Bach sonata.

"You play?" KT asked, surprised.

"Remnants of my misspent youth," the woman said. "My mother insisted it was proper for a young lady to play. I really just wanted to play drums."

"You should have had my parents. You could have played it all."

Gwen shrugged. "I believe we get the parents who can teach us the most, even when it's what we don't want."

"You play the hand you're dealt," she said, remembering Chance's words.

"Looks like you're folding," Gwen said with a knowing look.

"Damn it, I know. I'm letting everyone down. Bijou, my mom, Ashley, Chance, and myself." She stood up and began to pace. "But I'm just not cut out to be in the limelight like Bijou. Why do they think I should do that? Bijou can have the adoration. I just want to play my music in peace."

"So play your music." The woman nodded at the piano.

Fear froze KT mid-step.

Gwen came up to her and took her arms gently. She was a petite woman, but she radiated larger than life. "My grandmother once told me that the gift of life comes with a price; you have to live it to its fullest. To waste the gift is sacrilege. She used to say it was the same as taking someone else's life."

"Harsh."

She shrugged. "My grandmother wasn't a woman to mince words."

"Did she say anything about fear?"

"That it was nature's way of ensuring we didn't grow too bold."

"I don't think I'm in danger of that." KT took a deep breath and exhaled. So she was killing herself by not living to the fullest. "My mom would agree with your grandmother."

"My grandmother was a wise woman. She'd have liked you. She'd have given you this"—Gwen reached up on her tiptoes and kissed both KT's cheeks, in a French way—"and told you to walk bravely."

The thing was, she wanted to walk bravely. She thought about it as she headed home. People didn't understand how awful it felt for her to play in front of an audience. She didn't want it to be that way.

Chance's words flashed in her mind. Then play by different rules.

To release her music by herself seemed so hard. She'd have to get a production team, and someone to do cover art.

But her music would have a purpose instead of just sitting on top of her piano.

Growling, she pulled her hair. She needed space to think.

So, of course, she ran into her mother in the garden before she could escape unnoticed to her cottage.

"Hello, sweeting," her mother said, looking up with a smile. She wore a floppy hat you'd expect on a gardener and was using a hand shovel to dig up some flower from the bed in front of her.

She hadn't seen her mom since that night when she broke off the fake engagement. She didn't know what she expected, but it wasn't the pleasant greeting she received.

KT approached cautiously, waiting for the fallout. When her mom kept digging, KT finally exclaimed, "That's it? You're not going to lay into me, or give me a guilt trip?"

"You feel guilty enough already, Karma."

She sat cross-legged on the grass next to her mom. "So this is reverse psychology?"

Sighing, Lara laid aside the tool and stripped off her gloves. "Come here, sweeting."

KT took her mom's hand and scooted closer. Her mom angled herself toward her. "None of this was about torturing you. I simply want you to break out of your funk."

She wrinkled her nose. "Funk?"

"Darling, you've been in a funk since you were four years old, and it's my fault." Lara sighed sadly. "I've relived that moment in my mind so many times all these years, wishing I'd done something differently. I'd just been so proud of you and wanted to show you off. Then when you froze and got so upset, I tried to compensate for my blunder by letting you retract into a shell. I thought eventually you'd break free."

"You blame yourself?" KT asked incredulously.

"Of course I blame myself. I'm your mother. If I'd been less proud, if I'd reacted quicker, if I'd insisted you get back on the proverbial horse instead of coddling you . . ." She frowned. "I should have done something."

"Mom, this isn't your fault. It's my life."

"You can't honestly tell me you're happy with your life, Karma."

She had been, until she realized what she'd been missing.

Lara brushed aside KT's bangs. "I thought you'd made some headway with your music and Chance. What happened?"

She huddled into herself. "I got scared. Chance was right."

"Oh, Karma, everyone gets scared." Her mom cupped her face. "That's where people we love come into play. They hold our hands and help us get through the times we need support."

"You don't get scared."

Lara laughed. "My love, for the first year after we hit the big time, I used to vomit before every show. I blamed you of course—"

"Me?"

"Morning sickness." Lara grinned. "But truth of the matter was I only threw up right before going on stage. Anson, my dear, sweet husband, held my hair and rubbed my back and then we'd go on stage as if nothing had happened. I was always okay once I was on stage, but right before I was a mess."

KT shook her head. "I didn't know."

"Well, it's not glamorous." Lara smiled. Then she sobered and squeezed KT's hand. "I know performing isn't your thing, but making music is, and you're selling yourself short by not finding a way to do what you're meant to do."

"And if I still don't want to perform in the concert?"

"I love you no matter what, Karma. I can't say I won't be disappointed, but this is your decision." Her mom hesitated and then said, "Karma, isn't there anyone you trust enough to play in front of?"

Chance. She'd still been terrified but not so much that she'd completely frozen.

"He loves you," her mom said, reading her mind. She squeezed KT's hand. "If you asked him back, he'd come. With a small amount of groveling, of course."

"You think so?"

"It doesn't matter what I think, Karma. Don't you think he will?"

She remembered the way he'd looked at her right before he'd walked away, like he'd wanted her to come after him. She got to her feet and brushed off her butt. "I'm going to make sure he does."

Her mom smiled wide. "There's my girl."

**Since the night of the ill-fated engagement party, KT had come to three conclusions.

One: She was going to set her own rules from

now on. She may not want to be on stage, but she wasn't going to bury her music because she was scared. She'd figure out a way. And she was going back to teaching, starting with Ashley.

Conclusion number two: She needed a dress.

Which led to the third: She needed her sister, because no way was she going shopping alone.

Nellie said Bijou had gone to the coffee shop, so KT took a walk. Sure enough, Bijou sat at the counter in Grounds for Thought with Gwen and Lola.

Great—she could kill two birds with one stone. She marched up to them and pointed at Gwen. "Tell Ashley I want her ass on the piano bench tomorrow at the usual time, and I'm never calling her Spike ever again."

"Spike?" Lola asked with a lift of her brow.

Gwen didn't question anything though. She just smiled and said, "Welcome back."

"Thank you." She looked at her sister. "I was pissed at you but now I need you to help me buy a dress, so I'm over it."

Bijou nodded. "I'm willing to let you use my superior shopping skills for your own gain."

Then she shot up and hugged KT. "I'm so

sorry," she whispered in her ear.

KT sniffed back tears. "Let's just blame Mom and forget about it."

"Deal." Laughing, Bijou let her go. "So what do you need the dress for?"

Taking a deep breath, she let it out. "For the show."

Her sister shook her head. "There's no need to be in the show. I've taken care of my end."

She shook her head. "I don't think I want to know what that means, but I'm still playing, because it's a major part of the way I'm asking Chance to forgive me."

"A grand gesture!" Lola clapped her hands together. "I'll go shopping to support love."

"You'd go shopping regardless," Gwen said as she hopped off the stool. She clasped KT in a hug. "I'm happy you're back. Good luck shopping. You're in great hands, but I don't envy you."

Lola slung an arm over KT's shoulder. "Don't listen to her. This won't hurt."

"Much," Bijou added. She looked at Lola. "Something slinky, don't you think? Since she's trying to get her man back."

"If he's a true hero, he's going to want her, not what she's wearing. The dress is just going to come off anyway, if she apologizes right." Lola shrugged. "But it doesn't hurt to remind him what he's got."

"But we keep it simple, like black." Bijou tapped her finger to her lips, thinking. "And backless, because we can have her piano angled away from the audience. It'll help her if she isn't looking at them as she plays."

KT's heart melted at her sister's thoughtfulness. To cover the unfamiliar bout of sentimentality, she put her hands on her hips and scowled. "Guys. I'm right here."

"And we put her hair up to show off the line of her back," Lola said.

Bijou nodded. "But we need something different than a simple up-do, because she's a rock princess when all's said and done."

Lola snapped her fingers. "Bling!"

"Bling," Bijou echoed with a gasp.

KT shook her head. "What have I gotten myself into?" Groaning, she covered her face—and the happy smile stealing across it.

Chapter Twenty-seven

ALL OF SAN Francisco was in the concert hall. KT peeked through the heavy velvet curtains searching the crowd filing in. The audience milled about, laughing, chatting, and drinking. With the house lights up, KT could see their happy faces, all expecting a great show. All of San Francisco was waiting to hear her play, except the one person she wanted most.

Where the hell was Chance?

Bijou had promised she'd make sure he was there, but he wasn't backstage and trying to locate him in the crowd was like looking for a needle in a haystack.

One hand on her stomach, she lifted the other to her lips. She couldn't puke.

She might puke.

No—she shook her head—she wasn't going to puke. If she threw up, she'd probably get her dress messy and then Bijou and Lola would be pissed.

Where was Chance? She was only going through this for him, and he wasn't here? The jerk.

Okay, he wasn't a jerk, and she was doing this more for herself than anyone else. She wasn't going to be a coward any longer.

Her stomach clenched as more people filled the auditorium. Maybe there was something to being a coward.

"KT," Bijou said sharply.

The curtain was yanked away from her hands, and Bijou turned her around. "What are you doing?" her sister asked, surveying her critically. She pulled KT's hand away from her face. "Don't touch. You have makeup on."

"Where's Chance?" she managed to ask without swallowing her tongue.

Bijou looked sideways.

"That does not inspire confidence in me," KT said.

"Okay, I don't know where he is," Bijou confessed in a low voice. "But I've sent Lola to make sure he's here."

"You know I'm on first, right? My plan to win him back will have less chance of working if he's not here to hear me," she said, her voice escalating.

"Girls, are you fighting?" Their mother strode toward them.

Correction, the woman scolding them in her silver beaded flapper dress was Lara in all her glory. She had on stage makeup and her hair was piled on her head in an elaborate tower of curls with a beaded headband at her forehead.

The only imperfection to her was the frown on her face as she looked over KT and Bijou. "Why are you arguing? KT, are you okay? You look pale."

She waved at her face. "How can you tell under all this paint?"

Lara arched a brow at Bijou. "At least she's not catatonic."

"I guess that's a blessing," her sister said uncertainly. "Should I get Will to talk to her?"

"It couldn't hurt." Her mom leaned to look her in the eye. "How are you holding up, sweeting?"

"I'm going to puke, but I'll try not to mess up my makeup."

"That's my girl." Lara rubbed her arm. "If it helps, you look . . ."

When her mom didn't finish her sentence, KT offered her, "Green?"

"Stunning. Powerful." She tipped her head. "I love how those strands of rhinestones are woven into your hair. You're making your own style work for you, Karma."

She glanced at Bijou, who was the real mastermind here.

Her sister shrugged, and her red dress shimmered like fire with the movement. "I just worked with what I had. It's you pulling it together."

The lights backstage flashed to signal five minutes.

Her stomach clenched painfully, and her pits pooled with sweat. She swallowed the bile. "It's about to come apart."

Lara and Bijou looked at each other. "Will," they said in unison.

Bijou strutted off on her impossibly high shoes and came back almost instantly with her boyfriend, who was playing with her tonight.

When KT had told their parents she'd perform, their mom had offered Bijou her choice of musicians to accompany her. Bijou had only wanted Will.

"Hey there, KT," Will said in a soothing voice that belied his rocker image. "How's it shaking?"

"So hard it might fly to pieces," she replied. She gave him a flat look. "If you start quoting Zen bullshit, I'll aim my impending projectile vomit at you. It'd be a shame, because I actually like you."

He smiled and took her hand. It felt steady and grounding, giving her space to breathe. "We talked about this," he said in his horse-whisperer voice. "We'll seat you before the curtain goes up. You'll face away from the audience and close your eyes. You won't ever see the audience. They aren't there."

"She peeked," Bijou tattled.

"Karma." Her mom sighed.

"I couldn't help it," she said in a small voice.

"It's okay," Will assured her. "If you panic, just breathe. You can do this. I heard you play. KT, you're amazing."

She nodded, not believing it.

The lights flickered in warning.

"Oh geez." She gripped Will's hand.

"Let's sit and get settled." He led her to the piano bench. "Put your hands on top. Ground your-

self. This is where you belong. This is home."

Sitting and being off the unstable shoes did a lot to settle her. She closed her eyes and took deep breaths.

Will put her hands on the keys, and something in her eased. His hands fell away and he whispered, "This is it, KT. Play like you play for yourself. Play for the love of it."

Play for love. For Chance.

She could do that. He'd be here—her heart was sure of it.

Eyes still closed, she ran her fingers over the keys, warming them up. She heard the stir of the curtains and the drone of the audience hushing into a murmur and then silence.

She ran her fingers over the keys, stumbling. She froze, opening her eyes and staring at black and white.

The crowd was completely silent.

Her heart sounded too loud, echoing in her ears. She swallowed, twice, and again, willing her fingers to get going.

She couldn't chicken out. She couldn't let everyone down.

This was home. A crew of expert piano movers had even brought her own Pleyel to the concert hall. She had to do this.

No—she wanted to do this. For her mom, for Chance, but mostly for herself.

Her fingers ran over the keys again, and then she began to play.

She could hear the hesitancy in her music. She shook her head and closed her eyes and played.

The audience disappeared. In her mind, she pictured Chance leaning on the edge of her piano, watching her with awe and love.

Love.

He'd loved her a long time. Not from the first moment, maybe—that'd been lust. But he wouldn't have bought that ring for her if he hadn't meant it.

She'd been such a scared fool.

Without thinking about it, she transitioned her music into a different song that she'd written, one of loss and loneliness. She opened her mouth and began to croon indistinct sounds of loss.

But then she transitioned back into her concerto, hopeful and strong. The sounds became

words of love and encouragement.

She opened her eyes and met Chance's.

He stood at the back of the stage, in the shadows, watching her like a hawk. She sang from her heart, directly to his, telling him how much she longed for him—forever.

And then she heard Will's electric guitar segue into her concerto, and she softened her music the way they'd discussed. She stopped singing as Bijou's voice rose from the wings. Her spotlight dimmed and suddenly all the focus was on Bijou.

She waited until she was completely in the dark before she rushed offstage—one, to get away and, two, to find Chance.

He wasn't there.

Looking for him, she ran into Ashley—literally. The girl staggered back, and KT reached out to steady her, ready to cut off the tirade she knew the kid was about to launch into.

Except Ashley only looked at her with awe and reverently whispered, "That. Was. Awesome."

She'd almost forgotten she'd sent the kid an invitation. KT patted the girl on her head, held a finger to her lips, and moved further backstage in search of Chance.

Her mother stepped out from behind a velvet curtain and grabbed her arm. Without a word, Lara looked her in the eye and smiled proudly.

The knot inside her eased, and her legs wobbled. But she was willing to blame the ridiculous heels for that.

Her mother pointed to the dressing room assigned to KT. With a suggestive wink, Lara pushed her toward the door.

KT yanked open the door and looked inside.

He perched on her dressing table. "Nice performance, Karma."

Her eyes narrowed. "So glad you could make it," she said with saccharine sweetness.

He shrugged. "I had nothing better to do since my girlfriend dumped me."

"She didn't dump you." She put her hands on her hips, indignant. Her ankles wobbled and, with a muffled curse, she kicked off the damn shoes.

"I hope you aren't going to throw those at my head." He eyed them cautiously. "They look lethal."

"I should throw them at you." She glared at him. "You ran away from me! A relationship won't work when both parties run away, and I'm the runner here."

"Do we have a relationship?"

She strode toward him. "Now you're really pissing me off."

Chance looked at her warily, but she didn't give him the opportunity to say anything. "I've been trying to keep myself safe, but maybe I don't need to as much anymore," she said, "because maybe you could help me."

"So you want me to be your bodyguard?" he asked willfully obtuse.

She took his face in her hands. "I want you to hold my hair back when I puke and soothe my back."

Chance blinked. "That'd sound weird coming from anyone else, but from you it's sweet."

"Because I mean it." She knelt in front of him. "I've been happy living in my bubble, but you were right. I was scared. And now that I know what's on the other side of the bubble, I don't want to stay inside any longer."

"I was thinking of leaving San Francisco."

KT froze with a fear worse than her stage fright. "Are you still thinking that?"

He shook his head. "Ante Up convinced me we should stay. And I got a job. I've never had a job before, but I'm pretty sure it's bad form to leave before your first day."

"With Roger?" she asked, taking his hand.

"No, with his competitor Steve Hall." He looked at her. "The pig and I found an apartment, too. We made sure there's room for a big-ass piano."

Her heart swelled. She kissed his hand twice as she tried to get herself under control. Then she looked up into his eyes and said, "Marry me, for real. Nothing pretend, not temporary. You and me and our pig forever."

He lifted her up to her feet, which was a good thing because she wasn't sure she'd be able to get off the floor by herself in the tight dress Bijou and Lola had picked out. He laid his hand along her face and said, "I wondered how long it'd take you to ask."

"Bijou says I'm a slacker," she said softly.

"You certainly were this time."

She nodded. "A coward, too."

"I'd noticed," he said, drawing her to him.

"But I'm done with that now." She took a deep breath. "I've been thinking of releasing my music under my own label."

"That's a genius idea."

She knocked his shoulder. "Don't gloat."

He smiled. "It's difficult not to."

"Are you going to be smug forever?" Truthfully, she didn't mind if it meant seeing that endearing smile for the rest of her life.

"Just for a little while."

"Well, it's good I love you, then."

He stilled.

She batted her eyelashes, which were thick with goop. "Didn't I mention that?"

"Actually, I don't think you did."

She looked into his eyes and sang

Strange dear, but true dear,
When I'm close to you, dear,
The stars fill the sky,
So in love with you am I.

He dropped his forehead against hers, squeezing her tight. "My mom used to sing that to my dad."

"And now we're going to carry on the tradition in our family."

His grip tightened on her. "I love you," he whispered huskily, his head buried in the crook of her neck.

Then he let her go so abruptly she stumbled backward. Reaching into his pocket, he scrounged for a moment before pulling out her ring.

She held her hand out wordlessly, and he slipped it back on, where it belonged.

Epilogue

ROSALIND SUMMERHILL WAS never the bride.

Not that she wanted to be—precisely. But for someone who dealt in weddings, she was remarkably removed from the actual day's affair.

She leaned over the stair railing, a silent witness. Watching the Taylor household in the throes of pulling it together for KT's wedding, she wondered if it wasn't a blessing. By all things holy, it was noisy.

If she'd had to describe a wedding, she'd have cited candlelight and reverent music, hushed vows and murmured well-wishes. In her parents' house, no one ever spoke, and the hallways echoed with regrets.

An hour away from the ceremony and the Taylor house was rocking.

Music blasted through the house, a compilation of the family's songs and other rock greats. Guests were arriving, gathering around the bar. Laughter floated upstairs.

KT's outraged scream punctured the joy.

Frowning, Rosalind turned around and looked down the hall toward the room where all the women congregated around KT. No one came running out, but she had horrifying images of the wedding dress she'd designed for KT being ruined so she hurried to make sure everything was well.

"Is she okay?" she asked as she stepped into the room.

"Most likely," Bijou said, standing with the other ladies, a glass of champagne in her hand. "Olivia's in there with her."

"Foundation garments can be torture," Gwen said.

She'd met the funky pixie earlier, but she kept staring at her, marveling the way she pulled off the scarlet dress with her orange hair.

"It's the price you pay to make your man happy," the blond author in the silver sheath said. Lola was her name, if Rosalind remembered correctly.

The teenager — Rosalind still couldn't figure out whether her name was Ashley or Spike, or how she fit into the picture — looked up from the notes she scribbled into a notebook. "KT's just a drama queen."

"Amen to that." Grinning, Bijou held up her glass and all the ladies toasted.

"I heard that," KT yelled from the behind the closed door.

They all exchanged smiles.

There was a knock at the door and then a male head poked in. "Can anyone join this shindig? I have cookies."

There was a moment of squawking confusion. Then KT opened the bedroom door and poked her head out. "It's just Scott, for frick's sake. Let him in. He has cookies."

Scott and KT had been best friends for a long time, longer than Rosalind and Bijou had been. For as long as she could remember, when she came home from school with Bijou, Scott was always around. They used to whisper in the dark about him. He'd always been the hot older man.

Bijou winked at her, knowing where her thoughts were. Rosalind smiled unapologetically. Scott had been cute back then, but he'd grown into his looks and layered it with power. It was a heady combination, even recently married as he was.

"Cookie," KT ordered, holding her hand out.

"You'll mess up your lipstick," Bijou pointed out.

Her sister gave her a quelling glare and took the biscuit Scott gave her. "You're the only one who loves me, Scott."

"Actually, it's Celeste who loves you. I just wanted to see you in your underwear."

KT held her middle finger out to him. Then right before retreating back into the makeshift dressing room, she said, "Spike, did you put on dress combat boots for my wedding? I'm touched."

The teenager rolled her eyes, but a smile hovered at the edge of her lips.

Scott set the cookies down and picked up the champagne bottle to refill all the glasses. "Do you ladies need anything before I go join the zoo?"

"Is Julie downstairs?" Lola asked.

"She's checking the flowers one last time." He smiled, love softening his face. "You know what a perfectionist she is."

"You all know each other?" Rosalind asked.

Lola laughed. "Laurel Heights is an amazing place."

"Dali said all the world met at the train station in Perpignan, but he was wrong." Gwen discarded her grape vine. "It's Laurel Heights."

The bedroom door opened again, and Lara Taylor beamed at them. "Rosalind darling, Karma's ready for you."

"Thank you, Mrs. Taylor." She knew she was probably the only person in the world to call the famous Lara "Mrs. Taylor" but old habits and ingrained manners didn't die.

Mrs. Taylor eyed Bijou head to toe. "Bijou's dress is beautiful, Rosalind."

"Right?" Bijou said. "I look awesome. I'm sure to get lucky during the reception."

She glanced at Mrs. Taylor, who laughed as though Bijou had commented on the weather. If she'd said something similar to her mother, her mother would have been mortified. Not that she'd have said any such thing. There was a reason the British were noted for their reserve.

Olivia followed Mrs. Taylor out of the room, looking very satisfied. She came over to hug Rosalind—they'd met to confer on KT's underwear on special request from the groom. "She's all yours, and I need some of that champagne."

Rosalind murmured apologies to the group and went to attend to KT.

KT paced at the end of the room. The sun shined in through the window, lighting her hair like a honeyed confection. She wore a white silky robe, low heels, and an annoyed expression.

"Thank goodness." She rushed to Rosalind and hugged her.

"Why do I feel like it's not really me you're happy to see?" Rosalind asked with an amused smile.

"Probably because you know that I know you signal the last of all the torture." KT grabbed her, imploring. "Make it stop."

She laughed. "Just remember your lovely man waiting for you."

"Right." Frowning, she nodded. "Good point. Okay, let's get this done."

Rosalind went to the closet and pulled out the dress she'd hung there earlier. She pulled it out, giving it the reverent due all wedding dresses warranted. Taking it off the hanger, she arranged it on the floor. "Step in carefully."

KT shrugged out of the robe, revealing a beautiful red strapless bra and matching lacy cheeky panties. She must have sensed Rosalind's gaze, because as she stepped into the pool of material on the floor, she said, "I know. Chance likes the harlot look."

Actually, KT looked like a French aristocrat in the expensive lingerie, but Rosalind knew better than to say anything. She focused on gently shimmying the dress up KT's body and settling it in place. She buttoned it, double-checked how it lay, made sure it fit perfectly, and then nodded. "Look in the mirror."

They both looked.

KT looked perfect—a little rock star, a little princess, all KT. Lara had wanted lace but she'd capitulated that it'd be too fussy for KT.

Instead, Rosalind had picked a fine tulle that practically floated on its own. It was simple but stunning, with a light sparkle woven into the fabric. There were thin shoulder straps to keep KT from continually hiking up the bodice.

Rosalind looked at the end result of weeks of rushed work and felt an unfamiliar flood of emotion in her chest. She usually wasn't there to see her creations in real life.

More than that, this day was special. She'd been invited because she was Bijou's best friend—part of the family, Lara Taylor had said. She couldn't say how much that'd meant to her.

"I look pretty awesome," KT finally said. Then she laughed and threw her arms around Rosalind. "I know Mom and Bijou drove you crazy, so thanks for not making me look like a bag lady."

Laughing, she led KT into the sitting room, where all the women awaited.

They all gasped when they saw her.

Rosalind smiled. Exactly the reaction she strove for.

Bijou sidled up to her, slipping an arm around her waist. "You did good."

"I know," she said with a satisfied smile.

"Not that it matters. KT barely showers on a regular basis and she still managed to snag Chance. I think he likes her as she is," Bijou said drily.

"Chance is a good man."

"The best, except for Will." Bijou's face took on a glow.

It was lovely to see her best friend so happily in love. It was premature, because contrary to what people thought about her, Bijou was cautious and methodical, but Rosalind had already started designing her the dress to top all wedding dresses. Bijou would look like the diva she was.

Since the concert a couple months before, Bijou's stalled career had taken off. Her old label had offered her a new deal, but in a bold move, Bijou had opted to go with a smaller record company who offered her more creative control. She'd always been a go-getter, but since she met Will she'd become a force.

Rosalind couldn't have been happier for her. Bijou was a sister to her—certainly closer to her than any of her own sisters. And that was saying something, since she had five.

Bijou ran a hand down her glittery dark pink dress. "Thank you for making me look better than the bride, by the way. Bridesmaid dresses are usually so ugly."

Rosalind gave her best friend a flat look. "My

bridesmaid dresses are always lovely."

Bijou rolled her eyes. "Yours don't count, silly."

Mrs. Taylor clapped her hands together. "Ladies, shall we make our way downstairs?"

As everyone filed out, Bijou stuck a glass of champagne in her sister's hand. "Drink this now."

"I hate champagne," KT said, reluctantly taking it.

"You'll thank me when you see the crowd downstairs."

KT downed it then held the glass out. "Another."

Rosalind knew KT had made progress with her stage fright, but it'd been her companion for so long it was a hard habit to let go. But she'd finally decided to release her music herself. No one seemed to care that she had no desire to perform in front of crowds, least of all the critics, who loved the first concerto she'd just put out.

They filed out of the room, Rosalind trailing behind, observing like she normally did. She'd always been on the outside, even as a child. She usually didn't mind it—in fact she preferred to be left alone. But sometimes . . .

"Come on." Bijou took her hand, drawing her into the party. "I saved you a spot up front with Will."

They walked with the noisy gaggle, all the way downstairs. Rosalind hugged Bijou, checked KT one last time, and then went to sit next to Will.

Bijou's boyfriend smiled at her. "They all ready?" he asked.

"Wait until you see her."

"She always looks stunning," he said like a man truly in love.

"Yes, but now she's in one of my dresses." Not that she expected a man to understand. It took a rare woman to know what exactly she was getting with one of Rosalind's dresses, and she preferred it that way.

Bijou's mom had said there weren't that many people attending, but it certainly looked like it. Lara Taylor never did things halfway though.

A piano commanded everyone's attention. Rosalind looked, noting with shock it was the goth girl Ashley—or Spike—playing. Lara and Anson began to sing a ballad as they walked down the aisle arm-in-arm. Bijou joined in as she strutted after them.

There was a titter of laughter. Rosalind craned her neck and chuckled when she saw the little pig trotting down the aisle wearing a bow tie. He went directly to Chance's side and stood there, waiting.

The guests hushed.

Rosalind broke out in goosebumps as everyone gasped at the first sight of KT. That was the proper reaction.

KT didn't look as pleased. In fact, she looked pale. She'd been determined to walk herself down the aisle, but Rosalind wondered if it wouldn't have been better to have Anson help her.

Chance, his heart in his eyes, left his spot and strode toward her. He stopped halfway and held his hand out.

Love lighting her eyes, she reached out to him and met him halfway.

Rosalind sighed. One day, maybe.

The ceremony was blessedly short. Will kissed her cheek when it was over and went to find Bijou, probably to shag in a hidden corner. She was about to go in search of a glass of wine when her phone vibrated.

It was London—her parents' number.

She made a face at the screen. It was probably her dad, calling to berate her choices in life. He'd never had a comfortable relationship with any of his daughters, but he and Rosalind had been especially like oil and water. It'd made the decision to move to the States to study fashion that much easier.

She hadn't been back to London in ten years.

She looked at her phone. Pick it up and subject herself to his ongoing tyranny, or enjoy the moment?

Enjoy the moment. Duh, Bijou would add.

Rosalind was about to put the phone away when the call ended and another one came in, this time from her oldest sister Beatrice.

Beatrice never called her.

Frowning, curious, she answered. "Bea?"

"Why haven't you been answering?" her sister said.

No hello. No how are you. Typical. "I'm busy right now, so if this is just a social call—"

"Rosalind, Father died. You need to come home."

Discover the book that launched Kate's best-selling Laurel Heights series, Perfect For You...

From Perfect For You (Laurel Heights #1)...

Graphic designer looking for hot sex.

Freya Godwin shook her head and crossed out the sentence. Too blatant. That may be what she was looking for, but maybe she should be a touch more subtle. She didn't want every freak in San Francisco to respond to her ad.

Doodling faceless lovers entwined in different passionate embraces, she thought about what she really wanted. Finally she scribbled:

Female web designer seeking inspiration in order to complete a very important project. Bring your muse to share.

Lame. Accurate, sure, but it sounded desperate.

Who was she kidding? She was totally desperate.

Her office door slammed open. Flinching, she looked up to find Charles scowling in the threshold.

Hell. She quickly flipped the notebook shut. If he knew she was spending her valuable time working on a personal ad instead of the Sin City redesign, he'd blow a gasket.

"What the hell is this?" He waved sheets of paper in the air.

Maybe he'd blow a gasket anyway. "I can't see the pages with you flapping them around like that."

He strode into her office and slammed them on her desk. "Here."

Freya glanced down and mentally winced. The design was even more white bread than she remembered. She didn't need Charles to tell her that Sin City wasn't shelling out the big bucks for white bread—they were paying for buttery French pastry.

"Well? What the hell is this crap?"

It was the last throes of a web designer who hadn't felt an iota of creativity in over a year. But she just shrugged. "They're some initial ideas I had. They're not the final mock ups to show the client."

"Damn right, they aren't. If they saw this"— he stabbed a blunt finger at the printouts—"they'd run out of the building in horror. This is crap."

"Tell me what you really think, Charles."

Ignoring her, he braced his hands on the desk and leaned forward. "Do you understand what a coup it was for them to choose Evolve to redesign their website and revamp their branding?"

Yeah, she did. Evolve was well regarded in San Francisco's competitive web design field, but to call Sin City hiring Evolve a coup was understating matters. It was unheard of for a huge corporate entity like Sin City to go outside the biggie web design firms to a boutique shop like Evolve.

And Sin City was huge. They were Amazon and Facebook combined but for all things sexual. Store, blogs, chats, reviews, live video feeds— you name it. They even had their own publishing branch that put out several magazines in addition to a line of erotica for women. Compared to Sin City, the Playboy empire looked like a business run out of someone's garage.

"They didn't just choose Evolve, Freya." Charles's blue eyes burned with the zeal he was renowned for among his colleagues. His employees called it The Mania. "They chose you."

Because of the site she'd designed for a local sex toy shop two years ago. Back before her creative juices had dried up. "I understand, Charles."

"I'm not sure you do. If you screw this up, you're out of here."

Her mouth fell open. It took a couple tries before she could get any words out. "You can't fire me for one bombed design."

"I'm the boss. I can do whatever the hell I want. Especially if one of my employees blows the biggest opportunity this company has ever had." His eyes sparked with dollar signs. "This is our opportunity to play with the big boys. Maybe even go public. I won't let anyone screw it up."

"But—"

"And your work over the past year hasn't been up to your usual standards. I know Marcus bailed you out of the Accordiana job," he said bluntly.

She cut off her protest. She couldn't deny it—Marcus hadn't just helped her out with the design, he'd taken the crap she'd come up with and turned it into gold.

"If you can't perform, I can't afford to keep you. Just because you're Evangeline's best friend doesn't mean I'm going to make allowances for you."

"I can't lose my job." Her stomach lurched at the thought.

"Then I suggest you produce a design they fall in love with." He snapped his suit coat straight and turned to leave. At the door he looked over his shoulder. "I mean it, Freya. Fuck this up and you're out of here."

She winced as the door slammed shut. She couldn't afford to lose her job. It wasn't that she cared about herself—if she lost her paycheck she'd figure something out. But she wouldn't be able to support her sister Anna through college, and that wasn't acceptable. She'd vowed after the fallout from her parents' accident that Anna would never have to compromise her dreams like she'd had to.

That meant she had to produce a kick-ass design.

In the pit of her stomach she felt a spasm of

worry. She'd been off her game—she'd never felt such an utter lack of creativity.

She grabbed the notebook and opened it to her ad. She crossed it out and wrote

Artist in trouble. HELP.

The office door reopened and her best friend Evangeline poked her shiny blond head in. "You still alive in here?"

Freya slapped the notebook shut. "For the time being. Did you hear your dad?"

"Me and everyone else in the office." Eve closed the door and perched on the desk's corner. "I was just happy it was you and not me for a change."

"Why do you let him treat you like that?" She shook her head. Charles loved Eve, but it was tough love. "He may be your boss but he's your father too. If you stand up to him, he'll respect you more."

"I don't want him to respect me. I want him to leave me alone." She tucked her hair behind her ear. "Besides, you're the fiery one. You stand up to him enough for everyone. Except for today."

"I'm not fiery, and today was just strategic."

Everyone assumed that just because she had cinnamon red hair she had a temper to match. Not true. Not that much, anyway.

"Strategic?"

"I didn't want to aggravate him any more than he was."

"Hmm." Eve gazed at her like she didn't believe her. Then she picked up one of the discarded printouts. "Did you do this mockup?"

"Yes," Freya answered cautiously.

"It doesn't look like it."

"What does it look like?"

"Boring."

"It's just a mockup." She stretched to take the paper, crumpled it, and tossed it at the trashcan.

Eve leaned forward and picked up the notebook. "Interesting sketches."

Freya groaned. "Give that to me. I was just messing around."

"By drawing porn?" Her friend frowned as she flipped pages, faint parentheses lining the space between her eyebrows. "Artist in trouble? Are you writing a personal ad?" she asked in a hushed voice.

"Why are you whispering?"

"I wouldn't put it past Dad—I mean, Charles to bug the place."

Freya rolled her eyes. "Your dad is megalomaniacal but he's not that far gone."

"Did he or did he not threaten to fire you?"

"You heard that too?"

"Everyone heard. He's a beast. Especially given how he knows you're paying for Anna's college and can't afford to lose your job. I'd call him something worse but it'd be too disrespectful." She tapped the notebook. "But let's get back to this."

"It's nothing. A moment of insanity."

"If it's nothing, why are you blushing?"

"I'm not," she said even as she felt her face burn hotter.

"Right."

Eve stared at her with a narrowed gaze that was too much like Charles's for comfort. Then she said, "I have ways of making you talk."

"It's really nothing." Freya sighed. "I had the fleeting thought that if I found someone who made me feel like a sex goddess I'd be able to channel that newfound sexuality into the design for Sin City."

"And to find a sex slave you decided to do a personal ad?"

"I didn't say anything about a sex slave, and I haven't decided anything."

"Well, it's brilliant."

Freya blinked. "Excuse me?"

"It's brilliant. It's an inventive solution to a problem. You'll find a guy who'll help you get your sexy back so you can design something sensual and creative." She nodded. "It's just what you need. How long has it been since you've played footsy with a guy? The last one was Brad."

Brad. She sighed. "He was a good kisser."

Eve made a face. "He was boring. I rejoiced the day you broke up with him. You yourself said he didn't excite you."

True. She'd liked Brad, but once he proposed to her she'd realized she couldn't spend her life with him. Something was missing. Sometimes she was afraid the something that was missing was her.

"You know what you need?" Eve leaned forward, her gaze intense. "You need spicy."

"Spicy gives a person indigestion."

"You used to love spicy." She tapped the notebook. "Do the personal ad. It's the answer."

"It was only an idea in a second of desperation."

Eve shook her head. "No, it's a creative solution to a problem. It's old Freya shining through. It's exactly what I'd do in your place."

"Yes, but you have a habit of coming up with crazy schemes that backfire. Like that time you and I went to Napa for a day at the spa—"

"I just wanted to see what tipping a cow was like. How was I supposed to know that guy was out patrolling his pastures?"

"And when you decided we should take a road trip the summer after we got our drivers licenses even though we didn't have money or parental consent—"

"You have to admit it was a genius idea picking towns where the fire stations were holding free ice cream socials and spaghetti feeds. We saved so much money. And we met all those cute firemen."

"Yes, but we still ran out of money for gas and had to call our parents to wire us enough money to get home. Which only sucked because you said we should tell them we were spending the week at each other's house so they didn't know we were on a road trip."

Eve wrinkled her nose. "We did get busted that time."

"We got grounded for the rest of the summer," Freya corrected.

"That was unfortunate, but you can't deny you loved every minute of it. And I may have had the ideas, but you were the gung-ho one who acted on them."

True, and she did love those times. But that was before she had to take care of Anna.

Eve frowned for a brief moment before she lifted her determined chin. "No one's going to get grounded this time. The fact of the matter is you are desperate, and desperation requires drastic measures. Also, I'd like to point out that this was originally your idea, not mine."

"It's years of your bad influence." Freya sat back in her chair. "People always assume you're the angelic one, with your cherubic looks. But it's the innocent looking ones who're the most diabolical."

"I know," her friend said with a proud smile. "But I try to use my powers for good."

Freya sighed. "I don't know, Eve."

"Remember how you always wanted to be a bohemian artist? After high school, you planned to go to Paris, live in an attic, wear lots of scarves, and smoke Gauloises. But when your parents died, it all changed."

"I remember." Familiar sadness filled her chest, and Freya rubbed her heart to try to ease it. It'd been years since her parents' accident, but she still missed them every day.

Eve took her hand. "You had to be responsible because you had to take care of Anna, so you started to play it safe. Somewhere along the way, you lost yourself. You've dried up."

"It really is that bad, isn't it?"

"Freya, you're turning into a human Sahara. You've become as bland as your designs." She waved at the trashcan.

"Ouch." She winced, but she couldn't dispute that bland was exactly how she felt.

"Don't get me wrong. You don't look bland. You're hot. The programmers eye your butt every time you walk through the office. Those pencil-thin cords are great." Eve sighed in longing. "I wish I could wear pants like that. If only I were tall like you."

"5'5" is tall for women. You shouldn't compare yourself to me. 5'11" is abnormal."

"I wish I could be abnormal like a supermodel too. At least your chest is flatter than mine. It'd be terrible if I had to hate you for that too."

"Thank God for that."

"I'm just saying you need to shake things up before you're tempted to buy white cotton underwear."

"I'm not that far gone."

"You're one step away from it." Eve waved the notebook. "This is what's going to save you. Do it."

Freya sighed. "I'm a visual artist. I suck at writing."

Eve flipped the notepad to a fresh page and extended a hand. "Pen."

Handing one over, she watched Eve frown at the blank page before scribbling a few lines. Then her friend held out the notebook. "Here."

Taking a deep breath, Freya looked it over:

Fiery goddess in search of the perfect god. Soar with me through clouds, frolic under the stars, hand me the moon for my own. Mortals need not reply.

She blinked and reread it. Not a blatant I want you to give me hot sex but it hinted that she wanted to share sensual pleasures, sex or otherwise, without sounding desperate.

More than that, reading it stirred something inside her. It took her a moment to pinpoint that the feeling was excitement. "This is actually kind of good."

"I know," Eve said modestly. "It's perfect for you. Promise me you'll use it."

Nerves set her stomach lurching again. But Eve was right—instinctively she knew she had to do something big to move out of the corner she'd backed herself into. "I'll do it."

"Then my work here is done." Her friend hopped up.

"What would I do without you?"

"That's too horrible a fate to even contemplate."

Eve tugged one of Freya's curls. "Good thing for you you're stuck with me."

"Yeah, good thing."

Legend of Kate

Kate has tangoed at midnight with a man in blue furry chaps, dueled with flaming swords in the desert, and strutted on bar tops across the world and back. She's been kissed under the Eiffel Tower, had her butt pinched in Florence, and been serenaded in New Orleans. But she found Happy Ever After in San Francisco with her Magic Man.

Kate's the bestselling author of the Laurel Heights Novels, as well as the Family and Love and Guardians of Destiny series. She's been translated into several languages and is quite proud to say she's big in Slovenia. All her books are about strong, independent women who just want love.

Most days, you can find Kate in her favorite café, working on her latest novel. Sometimes she's wearing a tutu. She may or may not have a jeweled dagger strapped to her thigh...

29516993R00213